About the Author

Born in London in 1939, Michael Moorcock has won international fame as a writer of fantasy and satire.

He began his career at the age of sixteen as editor of *Tarzan Adventures* and *Sexton Blake Library*; later *New Worlds* magazine became under his guidance a springboard for the finest contemporary talent.

He has published over seventy titles, received a Nebula Award in 1967 for *Behold the Man*, the Guardian Fiction Prize for *Condition of Muzak* in 1977, the World Fantasy Award and John W. Campbell Award, 1979, for *Gloriana*. *The War Hound and the World's Pain* was runner-up for the Science Fantasy Award in 1982.

Michael Moorcock lives mainly in London.

THE DISTANT SUNS

**Michael Moorcock
and Philip James**

**Illustrated by
Jim Cawthorn**

NEW ENGLISH LIBRARY
Hodder and Stoughton

Copyright © 1975 by
Michael Moorcock and
Philip James

Illustrations copyright © 1975 by
Jim Cawthorn

First published in Great Britain in
1975 by Unicorn SF

First New English Library paperback
edition 1989

03926373

British Library C.I.P.

Moorcock, Michael, *1939–*
    The distant suns.
    I. Title   II. James, Philip, *1929–*
823'.914[F]

ISBN 0-450-50104-3

Printed and bound in Great Britain
for Hodder and Stoughton
paperbacks, a division of Hodder
and Stoughton Limited, Mill Road,
Dunton Green, Sevenoaks, Kent
TN13 2YA (Editorial Office:
47 Bedford Square, London
WC1B 3DP) by Cox and Wyman
Limited, Reading, Berks.
Photoset by Rowland
Phototypesetting Limited,
Bury St Edmunds, Suffolk.

INTRODUCTION

Anyone reading a paragraph or two of this book will probably realise at once that it is untypical, even of my few true sf stories. I hope this introduction will offer some illumination and explain why, for better or worse, I have a stronger affection for this simple piece of didacticism than for many other of my books.

In 1968 I was approached by the London editor of *The Illustrated Weekly of India* (part of *The Times of India* group based in Bombay), who told me that he and his colleagues in the firm were very concerned about the slowness of Indian society's acceptance of practical science and its benefits. He asked me if I would be interested in writing a serial for the weekly whose huge audience was unfamiliar with science fiction as a moral or didactic medium. His intention was twofold; first he hoped to develop an Indian audience for sf; second he hoped to upset certain hidebound ideas which, for instance, equated a technical education with the abandonment of traditional wisdom. I became fascinated and enthused by his idealism and agreed to try to write a story which would address a specifically Indian audience (if there is such a thing!). Originally I had merely intended to write a version of the book I was then about to start which was at that stage entitled *The Distant Suns* (and was later called *The Black Corridor*), but after a couple of discussions with the editor and having thought the problems through I thought it would be better to start from scratch.

Meanwhile *The Illustrated Weekly of India* found itself with a minor problem: none of their illustrators could produce appropriate pictures for an sf story. Did I know anyone who could help? I immediately suggested Jim Cawthorn.

Jim Cawthorn and I have collaborated in various ways since the midfifties. Jim's rendering of Elric, for instance, was done well before the first story was completed and seen by no one else, so that it's hard for me now to tell how much of my description was my own and how much was taken from Jim's pictures. A year or so later we also collaborated on our only Sexton Blake story, *Caribbean Crisis* (under the house pseudonym of Desmond Reid). While I find it almost impossible to collaborate with anyone else, Jim and I have always found it pretty easy to work together.

The Bombay editors liked the samples Jim sent them. They commissioned a cover and a number of coloured and black-and-white illustrations for each part. We planned to do about twenty episodes.

The content of the serial was decided by the needs of the magazine and the nature of the audience. The result speaks for itself. I wrote a complete outline of the story and had done about half of it before Jim Cawthorn (as Philip James) agreed to take on the weekly episodes when I became ill. My own opinion is that Jim's contribution is rather better than mine.

Whether readers of *The Illustrated Weekly of India* were happy with the result we never discovered. A political upheaval in Bombay produced a major change in the editorial staff (including the London editor) and we lost contact with the publishers. The new editors had, I gather, different ideas, but ran the serial to the end. Our sole attempt to sway the hearts and minds of a subcontinent was met by a mixture of polite bafflement and even boredom from the new people. They never told us what response, if any, there had been. They did not, however, commission a sequel . . .

Nonetheless I was glad of the chance to express my own idealism about India and to play a small part in one of her impressive social and political experiments. The use of the characters from the Cornelius stories – then appearing from various hands in *New Worlds* and elsewhere – was inspired by the notion of putting the same characters in thoroughly-different periods and backgrounds and seeing what happened. I don't think *The Distant Suns* contributed hugely to the Cornelius mythos, but it was fun to have Jerry as a conventional hero of space opera and show some of the other people in similar good and bad roles. My character, Professor Hira, the Hindu physicist first introduced in *The Final Programme*, was fortunately ideally suited for the story!

The serial was supposed to be fun, our homage to a certain kind of sf from the early years of postwar Britain which we had read in the Carnell magazines and elsewhere when we were young. I doubt if the book sheds any light on the rest of my work and I've never been much of a hardcore sf writer, but it was enjoyable to try my hand at the form and, if nothing else, to prove that I was wise to stick to kinds of fiction more familiar to me!

Since 1969 Jim and I have continued our collaborations (including the movie script of *The Land that Time Forgot*) but *The Distant Suns* remains one of the happiest. We hope you will enjoy it for its own sake.

Michael Moorcock
Munich, W. Germany
December 1987

CHAPTER ONE

She was ready at last.

Colonel Jerry Cornelius of the United Nations Space Command stared at her with a mixture of love and trepidation. Today was the day when he would, once and for all, bind his fortune with hers. They were soon to become inseparable.

It was New Year's Day, 2021 and the sun was just beginning to rise over the vast expanse of silicon-concrete that was the Gandhi Space Launching Site a few miles north of Gandhinagar, India's capital city.

She was ready for blast-off.

The product of sixty years of intense technical and scientific development; the product of a concerted effort by all the nations of the Earth, she was beautiful. And she was inevitable.

Her birth, thought Jerry Cornelius, had been inevitable since that day in October 1957 when the first artificial satellite, Sputnik I, was put into orbit by the Soviet Union. It had been inevitable since 1969 when the booted feet of the American astronauts first sank into the ancient dust of the Moon. It had been inevitable since 1980 and the first landing on Mars. It had been inevitable since 1985 and the first Russo-American mission to Venus.

She was a spaceship.

She was a gigantic spaceship, over a thousand feet long, larger than the largest ocean liner ever built, and her mission was the most breathtaking ever planned by the space scientists. Her mission was not to explore the Moon, not to visit Mars, not even to land on Pluto, farthermost of the planets that circled the sun. She had been designed to explore *beyond* the Solar System. She was ready to travel the vast depths of interstellar space – to journey billions of miles through the black, cold, silent vacuum until she reached *another* sun where she would explore the planets of the star men had named Alpha Centauri.

Alpha Centauri. Jerry turned his handsome head towards the sky but saw nothing save for the comfortingly familiar pink-tinged clouds of Earth. Alpha Centauri. A star so distant that it took a beam of light travelling at the rate of 186,000 miles per second over four *years* to reach Earth. And yet, perhaps even more astonishing, Alpha Centauri was a near neighbour to Earth, compared with stars such as Rigel, whose light now visible to the people of Earth had left the parent sun fifty years before Columbus discovered America.

Even Jerry, familiar since boyhood with the basic facts of astronomy and space science, could hardly conceive the magnitude of the project he was about to embark upon as he stared through the observation window of the Control Complex at the ship which was due, in a few hours time, to bear him into the unknown.

She was a fine ship, designed to meet every possible

eventuality during the course of her voyage, to withstand enormous heat and terrible cold, to operate effectively in the atmospheres of alien planets and at different gravities. She had been tested and re-tested. She had been tempered in the fires of Venus and the frozen methane of Neptune, hardened in the deepest oceans of Jupiter where gravity was twenty times greater than Earth's. And now she was being prepared for blast-off.

Helicopters buzzed around the case of scaffolding containing the ship. Tiny figures moved up and down her hull. Huge fuelling bowsers pumped in the nourishment for the nuclear reactor that was her engine.

Cornelius stood in a gallery overlooking the main Launch Control Centre and he watched the scores of men and women as they hurried back and forth across the floor, checking their instruments, making last minute adjustments to their consoles. Everything was calm on the surface, but there was a building atmosphere of tension as the moment of take-off came closer.

'All this, just to send three people on a journey.' The voice was soft, amused, and Jerry recognised it. He turned, smiling.

'Hello, Cathy,' he said to his wife. 'Did the medic check you out all right?'

Cathy Cornelius spread her arms wide. 'I'm as fit as a flea and ready to roll. No hitches so far.'

'No.' Jerry's voice dropped slightly and he frowned out at the spaceship that was to carry them to the stars. More than his own life was at stake – more than the life of his wife and the other member of the crew – perhaps the peace of the world was at stake. Not for nothing had the ship been christened *The Hope of Man*.

The world was on the brink of disaster.

Even though the United Nations had been working in accord for the past fifteen years; even though every nation on Earth was represented at the Council; even though war had been unknown since the late 20th century – still a crisis loomed. Already China was threatening to leave the United Nations and America was muttering about using a 'limited amount of force' to contain certain rebellious elements who were beginning to raise their voices throughout the world. The issues were clear enough. Essentially, there were two – Food and Living Space. There were too many people in the world. The planet was rapidly becoming overcrowded in spite of the efforts of the United Nations to implement birth-control, sea-farming, and all the other remedies conceived during the 20th century to cope with the problem. It was now clear that these remedies had not been implemented quickly enough. It was impossible adequately to feed and house a large percentage of the world population. And the hungry masses were preparing to war on the more fortunate, threatening to destroy the stability that had been so hard-won, planning to get what they needed by means of violence. And if this violence did at last explode, it would spread so rapidly that the entire globe would be plunged into a destructive war that might even mean the end of humanity.

There was only one solution that the United Nations could see.

If the world was overcrowded, then new planets must be found – new planets in new Solar Systems – which could support human life.

This was the responsibility which weighed so heavily upon the shoulders of Colonel Jerry Cornelius. It was his job to find those planets and find them as quickly as possible so that even larger passenger ships could be built to take colonists to the stars where they could begin a new life with plenty of space and plenty of natural resources on fresh, new planets. And that was why the ship had been called *The Hope of Man*.

It was a desperate remedy. It was a remedy that should not have been necessary. If more people had listened to the voices of the prophets and visionaries in the 20th century, then the situation might have been avoided. If people had learned to trust the new scientific instruments and methods that had been invented and discovered in the 20th century, if the politicians had been convinced that their use was of absolute importance, if the people had overcome their superstitions concerning scientific farming methods, birth-control, computers, mechanised factories, if the educationists had concentrated on familiarising people with the ideas of science, then perhaps the stability of the world would not now be threatened, and *The Hope of Man* would be about to embark on a simple exploration voyage, not on a critical journey to find a last-minute solution to the mess in which the world now found itself.

Jerry sighed. He resented the burden that had been placed on him by his immediate ancestors. They had spent so much time bickering amongst themselves that there was now no time to set things straight.

He put his arms around his wife and kissed her on the forehead. He smiled at her. 'It's up to us, Cathy, I hope to God we succeed.'

A deep, cynical chuckle broke from the throat of the short, thickset man who now approached them. 'Let 'em rot in their own mire, Jerry. In a few hours, we'll be out of it – out there where it's clean and cold and beautiful. I hate the whole damned human race. I'd be glad to see 'em blow themselves up!'

Jerry smiled and shook hands with Professor Marek, the other member of the team. 'Your bark's worse than your bite, you old rogue. You're really as soft as butter underneath all that hair.'

Wrily, Frank Marek ran his hand through his mop of black hair and tried to smooth down his unruly black beard. 'Well, you've got to admit, Jerry, it'll be a relief to get away from all this talk of war and rumours of war.'

'In a way,' Jerry agreed, 'but one still feels – well – *involved* in it. It *is* almost like deserting the sinking ship in one way . . .'

'Deserting a ship in mid-ocean to go and look for land,' Cathy reminded him. 'It's not quite the same thing, is it, Jerry?'

'I suppose not.' The chronometer on his wrist suddenly bleeped. 'Oh, oh – that's the signal. We've got the worst ordeal of all to face now. It's time to meet the gentlemen of the Press!'

They entered the elevator that would take them down to ground level and the Press Room.

Behind them the sun suddenly touched the metal of the spaceship and turned it a blinding gold.

CHAPTER TWO

'Could you explain a little about the ship's "brain", Professor Marek?' asked the representative of the Swedish *Aftonbladet*. 'Is it true that the ship itself can actually think?'

'The ship is what we call a "sentient vehicle", yes,' Frank Mark said as he sat with his two companions in the deep comfort of the couch, completely surrounded by reporters, cameramen and photographers. 'This means that it behaves in many ways like an animal – reacting to danger instinctively. Essentially its brain is a highly sophisticated computer. This is linked to what you might call a "central nervous system" – the computer is aware of every function of the ship and at the first sign of anything – however tiny – going wrong, it will act to correct the fault. In some ways you could say that we will be travelling in the belly of an immense space-going whale – but a whale that possesses certain superhuman faculties!'

'And what about the atomic engines?' asked the *Pravda* correspondent. 'Are they completely safe?'

'As safe as any reactor can be,' replied the professor.

'And this new method of covering the distance in a matter of weeks.' The interviewer for the BBC directed his tiny ring-mike at Jerry Cornelius. 'I thought Einstein had proved that it was impossible for a spaceship to exceed the speed of light, Colonel Cornelius.'

'Einstein's reasoning is not, as far as we know, at fault,'

Jerry smiled. 'The ship employs a device known as a "Space-warp", rather difficult to explain without recourse to some pretty complicated mathematical theorems. Essentially it has the effect of bending space – of folding space in on itself like a blanket, so that instead of travelling from one edge of the blanket to another in a linear way, we pass through the folded blanket to reach our objective.' Jerry laughed at the puzzled expressions on the newsmen's features. 'I told you it was hard to grasp, but the idea has existed for nearly a hundred years – only recently have scientists been able to come up with a means of making that idea reality. Therefore, though it would take us five or six years – perhaps much more – to reach Alpha Centauri by the *linear* method, we take advantage of the fact that space is *curved* – we make a short-cut, in fact – and should get to the new star system in five or six *weeks*.'

'But this Space Warp device . . .' said the interviewer for TV Peking '. . . it has not been fully tested, I gather?'

'It's been as well tested as possible,' Cathy said, 'but obviously it hasn't been possible to test it under the conditions in which it will be used.'

'So there is something of a risk?' said *The Times of India* correspondent.

'I suppose so,' Cathy answered. She brushed a stray lock of auburn hair from her face.

'Would you say there was considerable danger?' asked the reporter from *The New York Herald Tribune*.

'We'll be able to tell you the answer to that one when we get back, gentlemen.' Jerry smiled and got up. 'Now, if you don't mind, I think we're due for our final briefing. See you again in six months time, I hope.'

The three astronauts made their way through the babble of last minute questions out of the Press Room and down the bare, white corridor to the Briefing Room.

'Phew!' Jerry mopped his forehead. 'What an ordeal!'

'I thought you answered the questions pretty well consider-ing how difficult it is to explain to the layman just how a ship like *The Hope of Man* works,' Cathy said.

'They're right about the Warp, though,' Marek added.

8

'Those newsmen really sense where the hitch is, don't they? If the Warp goes wrong – we're in real trouble!'

'We could be finished,' Jerry agreed. 'But worse still – it might mean the finish of the world.'

In sober silence they entered the Briefing Room. Field Marshal Hira was waiting for them. A tall, elegant man, his expression was grim. 'Well,' he said, 'this is it. I hope you haven't decided to change your minds.'

Jerry grinned. 'It would be all the same if we had, wouldn't it?'

'Well, I don't need to tell you how desperate things are getting. The crisis is building virtually day by day. Even our most optimistic people at the UN think the balloon will go up within the year. Unless you can find at least one new planet that will support human life and return to tell us about it, I don't think there's much of a chance of averting disaster. One piece of good news from you, and it will give everybody something else to thing about – will channel all that anger into something positive. There's nothing else to say – except Good Luck.'

Hira shook them all by their hands, patted their backs and escorted them into the next room where their kit had been laid out.

As they were helped into their spacesuits, Jerry glanced at the chronometer on the wall. Just over an hour to go before blast-off. There was a tight feeling in the pit of his stomach.

Cathy smiled at him encouragingly, but even that could not change the mood of introspection into which he had fallen. He had volunteered for this mission three years before – volunteered in a spirit of idealism, because he had wanted to do something useful for humanity. But only now were the full implications dawning on him. Cathy had volunteered in the same spirit – that was how he had met her, fallen in love with her and married her in the space of a few months – and he knew that she, too, was suddenly feeling the weight of her responsibility.

Frank Marek on the other hand was whistling cheerfully as

the assistants zipped him up in his bulky kit. Jerry wished he had the professor's healthy cynicism about the venture. But it was too important to him.

Trained as a biophysicist, Cornelius had spent his early years involved in research into nutrition, but the work had become steadily less satisfying and he had entered the United Nations Air Service and trained as a pilot flying planes of emergency rations to out-of-the-way parts of the globe. But still the itching sense of unfulfilment – still the sense that he was not making the best use of himself, either of his own benefit or for society's. At last the opportunity had arisen for him to join the Space Service. He had served on various missions to the nearer planets, doing valuable research and feeling fairly satisfied. But it was not until the Alpha Centauri mission had come up that he had realised that this was what he had been waiting for all his adult life. The training had been intense, gruelling, sometimes heartbreaking, but it had been worth it. Cathy, trained as an ethnologist, had had a similar background, had studied ecology, also had experience of expeditions to Mars, Ganymede and Neptune. Marek, however, was something of an unknown quantity. A brilliant physicist, he had headed the team which had made the first descent into Jupiter's Red Spot and had also been the first to unravel the secret of the Rings of Saturn. He appeared to have no nerves at all and certainly understood a great deal more about the detailed workings of the ship than the others – yet he did not seem particularly interested in the mission. Perhaps that was just the front he presented to the world, Jerry decided.

At last they were completely clad in their spacesuits and, carrying their heavy helmets under their arms, they made for the door that led out to the space field itself.

The space field gleamed in the rays of the sun and the ship, still in its cage of steel girders, seemed a very long way away. The fuel bowsers had gone, the helicopters had vanished, the technicians had left. Everything seemed very quiet and still as they began the long walk across the silicon-concrete expanse, watched by a score of TV cameras, watched by the dozens of team members at work in the Control Complex – watched by the world.

The world watched. The world waited.

Upon the success or failure of this mission depended the fate of all mankind.

Jerry turned back once to look at the Complex, turned his head to stare up at the looming bulk of *The Hope of Man*, and he drew a deep breath, put his arm around Cathy's shoulders, winked bravely at Frank Marek and grinned.

'Here we go,' he said. 'All aboard, ladies and gentlemen – next stop – the stars!'

CHAPTER THREE

The three astronauts lay back in their acceleration couches waiting tensely for the final countdown that would launch them into the void of interstellar space.

Jerry Cornelius turned his helmeted head and looked at his wife, reached out a bulky, gloved hand to touch her once on the arm and smile.

Around them were the banks of screens, switches, indicator boards, knobs, dials, buttons, levers and all the rest of the electronic and nucleonic paraphernalia needed to run the most complex machine ever devised by man. As if operated by ghostly, invisible hands, buttons depressed themselves, switches clicked on or off, lights flashed, as the ship's delicate cybernetic system tested itself out. Only the set of controls to the left of the great semicircular bank seemed dead. These were the controls for the mysterious Warp Drive that would take the ship into something the scientists vaguely called 'hyperspace' where the journey would take weeks rather than years.

Nothing was known of hyperspace and the Warp was the one unknown factor that threatened danger for the expedition.

Frank Marek's harsh tones now issued from his helmet microphone. 'We're all set to go, gentlemen.'

He was speaking to Central Control whose job was to push the button that would send the ship into space.

'Get ready for the final countdown,' came the voice over the intercom. 'Thirty seconds to go.'

Jerry suddenly felt relaxed. There was no turning back now. The decisions were out of his hands – at least until they reached Alpha Centauri. The tension went out of him and he studied the indicators almost absent-mindedly.

'Twenty seconds to go.'

Cathy Cornelius shifted in her seat.

'Ten seconds to go. Prepare for ten second countdown.

Jerry thought of Earth. He thought of the overcrowding, the threat of starvation and war and the ultimate catastrophe. He thought of the friends he might never see again. And yet the strange sense of calm still filled him.

'TEN.' The volume increased as the final countdown started. It seemed to echo through his skull.

'NINE.'

Automatically – operated by the ship's cybernetic system – relays clicked on the control board.

'EIGHT.'

A television screen – one of thirty ranged above the control panel – flashed red – MAIN ROCKETS – MAIN ROCKETS – MAIN ROCKETS . . .

'SEVEN.'

Jerry saw Professor Frank Marek's hands grip the sides of the acceleration couch.

13

'SIX.'

A muted murmuring came from the bowels of the ship and Jerry sensed a faint tremor.

'FIVE.'

Another screen began to flash green. ALL SYSTEMS AT GO – ALL SYSTEMS AT GO – ALL SYSTEMS AT GO . . .

'FOUR.'

The murmuring grew slightly louder. A spasm went through the spacecraft.

'THREE.'

Jerry drew a deep breath.

'TWO.'

A high-pitched whispering sound came and went.

'ONE.'

This was it.

'ZERO!'

The ship shuddered. Jerry felt his body pressed back against the acceleration couch, saw the screen flashing SHIP IN FLIGHT, heard a babble of sound over the intercom, felt a roaring in his ears. He took deep, long breaths as the pressure increased and all the sounds merged into one painful buzzing noise and his vision blurred so that it was impossible to make out details on the control panel in front of him. The ship was travelling so rapidly now that he had the equivalent of six times Earth's gravity pushing against him. But he was used to this – he had travelled through space before. A sensation of nausea filled him. His limbs felt like jelly and every bone and muscle in his body ached horribly. He knew that the others were suffering the same sensations.

And at last, mercifully, he blacked out.

When he came to, a feeling of well-being, equal to the feelings of discomfort he had experienced so recently, filled him. He knew that they had left Earth's atmosphere and were already in outer space. The TV screens were filled with faces – the faces of the technicians they had left behind at Ground Control. He loosened the straps around his space-suited body

14

and they drifted in the weightlessness of space. He unclipped his space helmet and it began to drift away from his head as if through water. He reached out and caught it and the action caused his own body to begin to rise from the coach on its own accord.

'Order to Ship,' he said calmly. 'Switch to half gravity.'

'Order implemented,' came the reply, and Jerry drifted to the floor once again, though he still felt very light, since only the equivalent of half Earth's gravity had been switched on.

He crossed to Cathy's acceleration couch. She was just opening her eyes. She smiled when she saw him and he saw her lips move, heard a muffled sound from within her helmet. He shook his head to indicate that he couldn't understand her. She smiled again and unclipped her helmet, drew it over her head and shook out her auburn hair. 'That wasn't too bad,' she said. 'I've known worse take-offs.'

'This ship's got all the latest luxuries,' Jerry grinned. He turned to see Frank Marek straightening himself on his couch and yanking off his helmet.

'I'm glad that's over,' Marek said. 'I hate these damned romper suits. They make me feel like a two-year-old baby.'

Jerry turned his attention to the screens showing their rate of acceleration, position in space, rate of fuel consumption and so forth. 'Everything looks as if it's going perfectly to plan. Let's see what Earth looks like.' He raised his voice slightly. 'Order to Ship – show view of Earth on Screen Eight.'

Screen Eight came alive and there was Earth, all blue, white and green. They were still close enough to the mother planet to make out details of her continents, main cloud formations and so on, but they were moving away rapidly. Now they were passing through the Moon's orbit, with their speed steadily increasing, already a hundred million miles from the Sun. A tiny distance in terms of the enormous gulfs that lay between the stars.

The Hope of Man, travelling at a tremendous velocity, well over a thousand feet long, a great, gleaming thing of toughened titanium steel, that had looked too gigantic on Earth, was a mere speck in space – a mote of dust drifting rather slowly through the cosmic vacuum – apparently of no significance at all.

And space itself was not friendly. Space did not offer the comforts of Earth. Space was vast and cold and impersonal, uncompromising. Space could not be controlled, could not be tamed, could not be consoled or harnessed. Space was infinite; it was dark. Space was neutral.

Stars occupied minute areas of it – clustered a few billion here, a few billion there, as if seeking consolation in numbers. Space did not care. It did not threaten, it did not comfort, it did not sleep, it did not wake, it did not dream, it did not hope, it did not fear, it did not love, it did not hate, it did not encourage any of those qualities. It could not be measured; it could not be angered; it could not be placated; it could not be summed up.

Space was there.

It was not large and it was not small. It did not live and it did not die. It did not offer truth and neither did it lie. Space was a remorseless, senseless, unarguable Fact. Space was the absence of time and of matter.

And through this void the tiny pellet of steel inched its way, travelling so slowly as to seem not to travel at all. It seemed a lonely little object.

The Hope of Man was now travelling at a rate of 52,568 miles per second and had not yet reached its maximum speed which was 180,000 miles per second – just short of the speed of light. Only in the all-but frictionless vacuum of space could it reach these speeds, and only in space could its crew survive these speeds.

Soon they had passed the orbit of Mars and the orbit of Venus and were travelling through the asteroid belt. This belt, made up of millions of pieces of rock, some more than fifty miles in diameter, ringed the sun. Earlier pioneer ships had been destroyed by the asteroids crashing into them, but *The Hope of Man* had been equipped to deal with them. At the first sign of any danger the whole ship radiated a screen of pure atomic energy which had the effect of vaporising even the largest asteroid.

Jerry Cornelius sat in his control seat watching the television screens. Every so often there would come a blinding flash of colour as an asteroid came too close to the ship and the energy screen destroyed it. It was beautiful to watch and Jerry was fascinated.

Everything was going as smoothly as had been anticipated. The ship held its course steadily, still accelerating, still among the familiar planets of the Solar System.

As the ship left the asteroid belt behind, Jerry decided to get his first real look at space.

'Order to Ship – activate main observation port.' He swivelled his chair at right angles to the control board and looked at the large circular control room. The wall of the ship seemed to flicker with a thousand points of colour and then gradually turned opaque and then transparent and Jerry stared suddenly at the blackness of space.

There it was. Infinity. And flung like a handful of diamonds on black velvet were the stars, bright and sharp and shining, their light undimmed by any atmosphere.

The stars. Offering what?

Peace?

Jerry pursed his lips.

The chance for the human race to expand – to colonise other worlds – to spread through the galaxy?

Statistically it was likely that there were other planets circling those distant suns – some of which could support human life, which were sufficiently Earth-like to be habitable.

But even if they were habitable, there was a question that few had bothered to answer.

What if they were already inhabited? What if creatures completely alien to Man already lived on those planets? Then there would be little chance of colonising them peaceably.

Would the old pattern of colonialism begin all over again except on a larger scale? Would the people of Earth spread out in their spaceships to conquer and exploit whole planets?

Would they solve mankind's present problems only to begin the cycle on a larger scale?

Jerry sighed. He prayed that if they did find inhabitable

17

planets they would not already be occupied, that they would not give rise to the old diseases that had plagued Man for centuries – the diseases of greed, of violence, of tyranny, of hate . . .

Catherine entered the Control Room and handed him a pressurised beaker containing vitamin concentrate. 'You looked depressed, Jerry. What's up? You've seen the stars before.'

He nodded. 'I was just wondering what we'd find out there, Cathy. You never know. There could be people like us on the worlds we discover. Scientists say it's possible.'

'In the universe everything's possible, darling,' she smiled. 'I don't think it's likely that we'll meet human beings out there, however.'

Frank Marek entered the room. 'I hope like Hell we don't! What a horrible suggestion. I've just got away from one lot. No, no – we'll be lucky if we find a planet that's even barely capable of supporting human life. We don't even know if Alpha Centauri has *any* planets yet!'

They were now passing through the orbit of Saturn and they could see the great planet clearly, as if below them – though essentially there was no such thing as 'Up' or 'Down' in space. The huge, purple-green sphere, surrounded by its rings of bright orange, yellow and blue, hung in the blackness, looking as much like a child's bauble as anything.

Frank Marek stared at the planet reminiscently as it disappeared behind them. 'There's a funny world,' he said. 'I nearly died there.' He shrugged. 'I went on three expeditions to Saturn, you know.'

Jerry and Cathy nodded. Marek had acted heroically on all three expeditions, according to those who had been with him. Thirty men had lost their lives attempting to explore Saturn, four spaceships had been lost for good.

Now Saturn was a diminishing dot in the left-hand corner of the observation porthole.

Jerry wondered how many would lose their lives in the exploration of the planets of Alpha Centauri. Of course the intention was not to land on the planets, but merely to check if any seemed capable of supporting human life, but there was still a possibility they might not even reach the star that was their destination. Jerry glanced at the controls that lay to the right of the main control board, the controls that had not yet been activated. The controls of the Space Warp. The time was coming close when they would be activating them.

CHAPTER FOUR

Jerry joined Cathy in their cabin. It was Frank Marek's turn to take first watch and Jerry was grateful. He needed the sleep, he needed the comfort of Cathy beside him, he needed the sense of peace that he always experienced when Cathy was in his arms.

They were nine hours out from Earth and accelerating gradually all the time.

'Pleasant dreams,' Jerry said to his wife. Her eyes were already beginning to droop. 'Order to Ship – cabin light out please.' The light dimmed. 'When we wake up, Cathy, we'll have left the Solar System behind. An historic moment – the first people to go beyond the orbit of Pluto and we'll be sleeping through it!'

'Right now I'd rather sleep than witness *any* historic moment,' Cathy murmured.

The bed modelled itself to their figures automatically and they were asleep at the same instant.

They were shocked awake by a bellow from the intercom. 'Hey! Are you two lazy good for nothings still asleep? It's half-an-hour past my watch!'

Jerry grinned. At first, in his daze, he had thought the ship itself was talking to him.

But it was only Frank Marek.

'Okay, Frank, don't worry. We're on our way to relieve you.'

Jerry sprang out of bed and went to the smooth wall of the cabin, passed his hand across a certain area and saw a shallow tray emerge from what had appeared to be a completely featureless expanse of metal. In the tray were a number of small dishes containing tablets of various colours. He took a magenta tablet and popped it into his mouth. He felt instantly more wakeful. The pill had contained his breakfast and his morning pick-me-up rolled into one. He moved along the wall and passed his hand over it again. This time a section of the wall moved downwards revealing a fully equipped shower. He stepped into the shower and washed quickly, stepping aside for Catherine to enter. Another motion of the hand and a tiny package dropped from the wall into his open palm. The package contained a fresh set of clothes, including the cobalt blue uniform of the United Nations Space Command.

'I'll see you in the Control Room,' he told Catherine, waving to her. 'Order to Ship – open cabin door, please.' The door slid silently upwards and he passed through, walking down the long, steel corridor towards the nose of the ship where the main Control Room was situated.

He entered to find Frank Marek leaning on the globular star-chart that occupied the centre of the room. This chart was actually a completely accurate three dimensional model of the region of space through which they would be passing in order to reach Alpha Centauri.

Marek nodded to Jerry wearily. 'Sorry to shout like that, but I'm bushed, Jerry. Must get some sleep. Beginning to feel dizzy.'

'Of course, Frank. Sorry I overslept. How are we doing?'

'We're on perfect course. Five hours out from Pluto. It's going to be your job to put her into Warp, Jerry. Think you can do it all right?'

'I've been trained for it, Frank.' Jerry patted the older man's shoulder. 'Don't worry. You'll wake up if anything goes wrong!'

'But I might be dead . . .' Frank tried to grin, but he was

evidently worried about leaving the job of Warping in Jerry's hands. 'Maybe I should take a pill that will keep me awake . . .'

'It's better to sleep normally Frank. You might be needed later – and it would be best if you're properly rested.'

'You're right. See you, Jerry.'

Frank Marek disappeared from the Control Room, half-staggering with tiredness. Jerry watched him go and then checked his chronometer against the chronometer above his head.

Another hour and he would have to activate the Space Warp.

Catherine joined him and they went through all the routines they had learned and re-learned on Earth. The ship was about to enter an area about which almost nothing was known – for 'Hyperspace' was merely a name to describe the limbo *between* Time and Space, that strange area that had no right to exist at all, that some called the Fifth Dimension.

The hour passed quickly. Too quickly for Jerry and his wife as they made preparations.

At last it was time to activate the Warp controls. Jerry switched on and watched the control board come alive with flashing lights, simulators and indicators. His instructions were to phase gradually into Warp Drive, but once the Drive had been set at GO, there was no turning back. The ship's programming would do the rest, would see them into hyper-space and, with luck, out the other side, relatively close to Alpha Centauri.

But the Warp had never had a true test. They might disappear forever into that limbo. A new, horrifying death might await them. A death that their minds simply could not conceive – perhaps an eternity of different deaths in that timeless, spaceless place!

Jerry took a deep breath and glanced at Catherine as he began to punch the instructions out on the control panel.

He knew that this might be the last time he would ever look at his beautiful young wife again.

And he was suddenly filled with a sense of sheer terror.

They were about to leap blindly into the unknown – go where no living creature had been before.

Quelling the terror as best he could, Jerry pressed the final button. Now the programme was locked into the computer.

There was no turning back.

CHAPTER FIVE

There was no turning back.

Jerry poised himself over the Space Warp controls, his face bathed in the multicoloured lights that flickered from the console. Beside him, Catherine checked the normal operations of the ship, reading out co-ordinates in a rapid monotone.

They were in the gulf between the stars – in the empty, black, aching void of interstellar space, with the Solar System behind them and Alpha Centauri four light years ahead of them.

But it would not take them four years to reach the distant star, Sol's closest neighbour. It would take them perhaps four weeks – perhaps eternity.

Now the cybernetic ship itself began to speak. 'Prepare for Warp Phase One.'

Jerry's index finger rested on the appropriate button.

'Six seconds to go,' sang the ship. 'Five – four – three – two – one – zero.'

Zero.

Jerry pressed the button and leaned back in his control couch, his eyes on the screens before him.

Nothing happened.

He glanced in puzzlement at Catherine.

Catherine had turned a deep, lustrous green; her eyes were

mauve, staring in astonishment. The screens which had showed the blackness of space now swam with hazy colours. Strange shapes seemed to form and reform on the screens. A high-pitched whine filled the ship.

Jerry felt nausea threatening to overwhelm him. The ship shuddered and groaned and Jerry's teeth ached horribly.

From somewhere a rasping voice said: 'Prepare for Warp Phase Two. Five – four –'

It was the ship.

Desperately Jerry forced himself to concentrate on the control board before him. His finger found the second button.

'– three – two – one – zero.'

He stabbed the button down.

His ears roared as if he was trapped in a gigantic waterfall. Bile rose in his throat and his eyes watered. A steady, rhythmic banging noise began to sound. At first he thought it was the ships engines. Then, he realised it was his own heart.

Catherine was shouting something. She was now bathed in a brilliant scarlet aura.

'*Jerry – Jerry* – look at the screens!'

He blinked and peered blearily at the screens. They were warping into the unknown regions of hyperspace. They were the first human beings to witness it. And it had a frightening beauty.

Space seemed to peel back on itself as great, blossoming splashes of colour poured through as if from the broken sides of a vat, merging with the darkness and making it iridescent so that sections shone like brass and others like silver, gold or rubies, the whole thing changing, changing constantly, erupting, flickering, vanishing, reappearing.

And the interior of the ship seemed to be subject to the same chaos that Jerry Cornelius witnessed outside it. The whole ship seemed filled with bright whiteness, the whole hull seemed to become transparent and against the darkness of the cosmos the spheres which began to roll by, flashing past like shoals of multicoloured billiard balls, were unrecognizable as any heavenly bodies Jerry had ever seen. Not asteroids by any means, not planets – they were too solid in colour and general appearance; they shone, but not with the glitter of reflected sunlight. And they passed swiftly by in hordes.

Moved by the beauty, astonished by the unexpected sight, Jerry couldn't voice the questions which flooded into his mind.

In the faint light that suddenly filled the ship, Catherine's silhouette could be seen in constant motion. The whining had ceased. The spheres now appeared on the screen and began to jump and progress more slowly. The picture jerked and one sphere, smokey blue in colour, began to grow until the whole screen itself glowed blue. Then it seemed to burst and the ship flashed towards the fragments, then through them, and saw –

'A star!' Jerry cried. 'We'll burn up!'

The ship seemed to plunge into the very heart of the star, into the mass of waving flames. The flames – the word hardly described the curling, writhing wonder of those shooting sheets of fire. The control deck was not noticeably warmer, but Jerry felt his temperature rise just from the act of looking.

A roar of enigmatic laughter seemed to fill the ship, then fade, and then everything was deathly quiet. There was no sound at all.

Jerry turned his head again slowly, searching for Catherine.

She sat on an acceleration couch, her lips moving silently, her eyes staring, and it seemed to him then that she saw and heard something altogether different from the sensations that filled him.

Painfully he reached out to touch her arm. But she did not notice.

He spoke her name.

'C-a-t-h-e-r-i-n-e . . . . '

The sound was a muffled echo, but she did not hear it.

'C-a-t-h-e-r-i-n-e . . . . '

Again no reply.

Then everything went absolutely black and Jerry felt he was alone – alone in the blackness of space – completely and utterly alone – drifting, drifting, drifting . . .

Somehow he had become separated from the ship.

He was drifting in arbitrary configurations. He could not

see. He could not hear. He could not speak. He could not feel. He could not smell. Even his sense of identity began to fade.

He made one last desperate effort to cry out. He uttered a soundless scream and emerald-green light blinded his eyes. He twisted convulsively and he was in the Control Room again.

Everything was normal save for the peculiar swirling colours on the screen. He glanced at the chronometer and then at Catherine who was leaning against her acceleration couch panting heavily.

'How long . . . ?' he began. It seemed to have lasted for eternity.

Yet the chronometer showed that barely three seconds had passed since he had thrown the Warp into Phase Two.

There was still a third phase – the final phase.

Cathy's eyes were wide with horror. 'We can't make it Jerry. We can't.'

He gritted his teeth. 'There's no going back, Catherine. We've got to put her into Phase Three – and soon.'

'But it's – it's – so terrifying!'

'We expected abnormal sensations. After all, we're entering a plane of existence that is completely alien to the universe we know.'

'It will destroy us.'

'We must take the risk, darling. We must.'

He reached out and grasped her hand as the ship began to speak again.

'Prepare for Warp Phase Three,' said the ship.

'No!' Cathy cried.

But Jerry detached his hand from hers and returned his attention to the control panel, every fibre of his being fighting the panic that threatened to overcome him, every element of his consciousness resisting the black madness that gnawed at the edges of his brain.

'Five – four – three – two – one – zero.'

Jerry's shaking hand depressed the stud.

Something like an electric shock ran up his arm. The

instruments danced crazily. The ship seemed to spin end over end. He felt as if he had left his body. A thousand fragmenting images of Catherine flickered before him.

A strange wailing sound filled his ears.

Around him the air was jewelled and faceted, glistening and alive with myriad colours, flashing, scintillating, swirling and beautiful.

And then a great sense of tranquility filled him – a feeling of peace as intense as the feeling of terror he had so recently experienced. He seemed to drift with the ship as if in a boat on a gentle stream in summer. He leaned back, his body relaxing.

He felt a cool hand on his forehead and looked up through sweet, golden light at Cathy. She was smiling down at him.

'Cathy . . . ?'

'Jerry. Can you hear the music?'

He shook his head.

'It's wonderful – unearthly – are you sure you can't hear it.'

He kissed her hand and smiled quietly. 'No. I wish I could. Evidently, everybody experiences different sensations in the Warp . . .'

'It's a mental reaction, isn't it. Something happens to your mind.'

'That's my guess – the sensations are so alien to us that our senses attempt to translate them into ordinary experiences and fail completely. Even now, we are not undergoing any sort of normal experience. We . . .'

The ship screamed.

The golden light became shot through with veins of ghastly green. The ship began to bump as if it passed over a deeply rutted road. There was a sound like the deep-throated bellow of a great brass gong.

The Control Room seemed filled with terrifying beasts – like the beasts of Earth's ancient mythologies. They roared and croaked and cackled, beating their reptilian wings and baring their ferocious fangs. Jerry hugged Catherine close. She was shuddering in his arms, her face pressed against his chest.

'Oh, Jerry – when will it stop? When will it stop?'

The ship swayed and shook so that everything in it seemed to jangle and rattle. Waves of intense cold and blistering heat came and went.

And then it was over.

The Control Room looked slightly shaken about, but was otherwise normal. Catherine seemed a little dishevelled, but none the worse for her ordeal. On the screens the colours had turned to soft, swirling pastel shades and the instruments showed that they were now passing through hyperspace at a subjective speed of 175,000 miles per second.

'My God!' Frank Marek came in. 'I thought I was trapped in a nightmare. That was the Warp, was it? I don't want to do that too often.'

He went to the main control panel and began checking the instruments.

'What's the matter, Frank?' Jerry noticed a frown on the older man's face.

'Sluggish responses in some places. You know how delicate the cybernetic system is – well, I'm worried. Just a minute. Order to Ship – please report any irregular functions in ship.'

'Irregular function in engine section six. New cadmium rod req . . . req . . . req . . . requir . . . quired. Irregular function

30

in cybersystem involving short-circuiting of synapse co-
ordinates in – in – in . . .'

Frank looked significantly at the other two. 'You know
what that means, don't you? Something's gone wrong with
the ship's brain. And we rely on that brain for all the main
running of the ship. Jerry – Catherine – we're lost in hyperspace – lost in a crippled ship.'

CHAPTER SIX

For a moment an expression of pure panic crossed Frank Marek's face and an hysterical note crept into his voice. 'Without the ship's brain functioning properly, we could be marooned in space until we die!'

'Calm down, Frank,' said Jerry Cornelius. 'Every conceivable emergency is allowed for. You know that.'

'But this is an *inconceivable* emergency, you fool!' Marek shouted. 'The stresses of entering hyperspace have thrown the cybernetic system completely out. That's clear enough, isn't it?'

Jerry gripped the older man's shoulder. 'The first thing we must do is to switch the ship to manual control. It's possible to navigate and land her without using the cybernetic system at all. We'll just have to work everything out on paper, that's all. It *can* be done, Frank.'

'I know – it can be done in *normal* space. But this isn't normal space, Jerry.' Catherine spoke quietly. 'Frank might have a point, you know.'

Hearing this, Marek seemed to calm down. 'Can't you see, Jerry? We depend on the ship to tell us when to phase into hyperspace and when to phase out. How can we rely on its information even if it is capable of giving us the information in the first place?'

Jerry nodded. 'Fair enough. But before we start to

speculate, let's just make a few proper tests. It will take time. We'll have to get down to it right away. First we must cut out the main brain and control the ship ourselves. This means keeping a constant patrol. While one of us patrols the ship, checking for any signs of malfunctioning, the others must inspect the brain itself and see if we can put the damage right.'

Marek rubbed his eyes with his stumpy hands. 'I'm sorry, Jerry. You're quite right. That – that nightmare as we phased into hyperspace – it threw me into a panic. I acted like a fool.'

Catherine put her arm around Marek's shoulders. 'We were all badly shaken up by that. Come on – let's get busy.'

'I'll make a tour of the ship,' Jerry said. 'You're more expert on cybernetics than me anyway, Frank.'

He left them isolating the main brain of the ship and cutting out its power. He climbed into his spacesuit and began the slow journey down the length of the ship, down the metal corridors of the crew quarters until he reached the big steel hatch. It bore a red, stencilled sign:

HYDROPONICS SECTION. PLEASE PERFORM ALL DECONTAMINATION FUNCTIONS BEFORE AND AFTER LEAVING THIS AREA.

Jerry spun the manual controls of the hatch. At length it swung open and he entered the decontamination cubicle, closing the hatch behind him. He switched down the little lever that would start the decontamination process – cleaning his spacesuit of any organic material that was likely to upset the balance carefully preserved in the section he was about to enter.

The light in front of him blinked red and then changed to green, indicating that it was safe to proceed. He spun the controls of the second hatch and passed into the soft green light of the Hydroponics Section. This section was effectively a large greenhouse in which the ship's vegetable supplies were grown. But, in fact, the section did more than that. It actually replenished the oxygen supply of the ship by natural methods. Tall, fernlike plants, especially mutated for use on board spaceships, grew in special tanks of chemicals which supplied

34

them with a carefully balanced diet of nutrients. It was like walking through some strange, artificial jungle – a jungle created by Science.

Jerry moved from tank to tank checking the instruments attached to the tanks, checking that everything was functioning as it should do.

At last he reached the end of the Hydroponics Section and was satisfied that the journey into hyperspace had not adversely affected their food and oxygen supply. That was something!

At the next hatch he underwent the same decontamination procedures and passed through into another short corridor before he reached another hatch. This one was marked simply:

ENGINES
BEWARE OF HARMFUL RADIATION
All personnel must don the appropriate protective clothing before entering this section. All other normal precautions must be taken.

There was a small locker near the door. Jerry opened it and drew a thin, membranous covering over his spacesuit. This was a specially treated protective shield that would resist normal doses of nuclear radiation. Next Jerry checked the instruments set into the door. The radiation count was not high enough to be especially dangerous. He unlocked the door and swung it outwards, climbing clumsily through in his two layers of protective clothing, and closing it behind him.

The engines were all housed in grey, featureless boxes. According to the instruments, these, too, were functioning reasonably well, though not at the power Jerry might have expected.

Jerry passed through the dimly lit engine chambers until he

came to the atomic pile itself. Although utilising all modern miniaturisation techniques, it was still a considerable size, towering over him, its top disappearing in the gloom of the ship's roof.

Jerry found trouble at last.

An emergency indicator was flashing wildly and now it became plain as to why the engines were not working at full power. The burnt-out cadmium rod, used to damp the reactor, had not been replaced. An emergency dampening procedure had taken place automatically and was attempting to hold the reaction down. Jerry had arrived just in time.

Swiftly, he switched over to manual control and began manipulating the handling tongs, removing the defective rod and replacing it with a new one. Normally the ship would have done this, but the damage to its cybernetic system had come just as it had been about to put things right.

Jerry continued his tour of inspection through the various sections of the ship. Sometimes he paused to make a close check, but nothing else seemed seriously wrong. He could not speak for the internal workings of the ship, for only the instruments on the Board in the Control Room could show what, if anything, was wrong. He turned and began to make his way back to the forward section of the ship.

CHAPTER SEVEN

The days passed swiftly on board *The Hope of Man* as the three people pored over their equations – equations that would have taken the ship itself only seconds to do. Meanwhile, Marek worked on the brain, testing all its functions over and over again until he was satisfied that it was working properly again and could begin the long series of tests, leading up to the moment when it could begin working at full capacity once more.

It was only when the cybernetic system was functioning properly that Marek relaxed. His face was set in lines of worry and concentration and there were deep rings under his eyes.

'I think she's okay,' he said at last. 'Two days to go before we're due to Warp into normal Space. It was a close thing.'

Jerry breathed a sigh of relief. 'You've done an incredible job, Frank. You've almost certainly saved all our lives.'

Marek frowned. 'I suppose so. I wouldn't like to have to go through all that again. Now I suggest we get as much sleep as possible. We'll need all our energy for the ordeal of phasing back from hyperspace. It's a hell of a way to travel, isn't it . . .'

Jerry laughed. 'I wonder if we'll ever get used to it?'

With the ship working normally they were able to catch up with their sleep. Tension on board *The Hope of Man* began to increase, however, as the moment for phasing back came closer. Would they make it? And would they arrive in the area of space they had aimed at? Nobody knew.

The moment arrived.

This time Frank Marek sat at the Warp controls and Jerry and Catherine watched him from their couches. The ship began to speak its instructions. Frank Marek pressed the button.

The sensations began again. A thousand hallucinations came and went in a few seconds as the ship entered the first phase.

Jerry heard voices in his head during the second phase. They were the voices of all the people he had ever known. The voices of his dead grandparents, of his stern father, Bruno Cornelius, the chemist, of his mother, of his sister who had been killed in the Lunar Base disaster of 2018 and then, unable to bear the terrible agony, no longer needing to control himself in order to operate the Warp, he blacked out as the time came for the third and final phase.

He blacked out, not knowing if he would ever wake again.

'Look, Jerry! Look!' Catherine's voice.

Jerry opened his eyes and it seemed to him at first that he was back on Earth, lying on his back beneath the summer sun.

Then he realised that the main observation port was open and he was in normal space. But it was like no area of space he had ever seen.

For there before him, glowing a fiery orange, were *three* suns – suns very much like his own, but very close together, forming a sort of triangle in the sky.

'Then we made it,' he said flatly, staring in wonder at the stars. 'Three suns – the suns that make up Alpha Centauri. A triple star!'

'Yes, Jerry, we made it.' Catherine said. 'But not without cost.'

'What do you mean?'

Catherine pointed to the far corner of the control room. Jerry peered into the shadows. Something was huddled there. A creature of some kind.

'What is it? How did that get aboard?'

'Look closer, Jerry,' Catherine said grimly.

And then he recognised the huddled, shivering thing.

'My God! It's Marek – Frank Marek!'

From Marek's twisted lips there came a high-pitched giggling sound.

'We reached Alpha Centauri, Jerry. We reached it. I got us there, didn't I . . . ?' The voice was Marek's, but it was also the voice of a small, demented child. 'I got us here, Jerry . . .'

'The strain of the Warp jump proved too much for his brain,' Catherine murmured. 'I tried to get close to him. Tried to get him to take a sedative, but he won't let me touch him. We'll have to handle him together. If you can hold him, Jerry, I'll give him a shot from the hypogun.'

Jerry got up and approached Frank cautiously.

'Don't touch me, Jerry, please,' Frank whimpered. 'Don't touch me. You know how much I hate human beings. You know I can't bear to be touched.'

It was then that Jerry saw the gun in Frank's gloved hand – one of the weapons issued to them in case they should encounter danger on any of the planets they explored. It was a laser-gun, capable of burning him to ashes in seconds.

Jerry paused, preparing to leap for the gun and get it away from the demented professor.

Had he come all the way to Alpha Centauri, risked the dangers of hyperspace, just to be killed by a madman with a pistol?

CHAPTER EIGHT

Marek giggled and motioned at Jerry with the laser-gun.

'You're as bad as the rest. The human race is like a virus. It has infected one planet – now it seeks to infect the entire galaxy. I'll have no part of it. You are a cancer, Jerry – you and your like. And I have a cure for cancer – I'll burn it out with this.'

The ship was hurtling towards the triple star that was Alpha Centauri. Light blazed and the Control Room was a mixture of intense brightness and deep shadow. Cathy stood tensely by the main control console while Jerry stood poised on the balls of his feet, staring warily at the space-maddened Marek.

'Marek – try to see sense. The hallucinations in hyperspace – they turned your brain. You're not rational. Please put the gun away, Marek.'

'Shut up! You're my enemy. You – with your stupid ideals. Don't you realise the reason I came on this expedition? To be *alone*! To put four light years between myself and the rest of the human race! I no longer need either of you now!'

Suddenly Cathy shouted: 'Our speed! We're travelling too fast!' She was pointing at the speed indicators.

Marek glared at her. 'What does it matter if – ?'

Jerry sprang.

He grasped the wrist of the hand holding the gun and forced

41

it back, his face close against Marek's. The crazed eyes glared directly into his. The madman's finger squeezed the trigger and a beam of concentrated light left the gun and seared into the ceiling of the Control Room.

Desperately Jerry twisted the wrist. Marek's bearded face grimaced and his teeth clashed a few centimetres from Jerry's throat, his other hand clawing at Jerry's chest. Jerry's right hand grasped the barrel of the gun and wrenched it from Marek's grasp. He flung himself backwards, threw the gun to Cathy and then leapt forward to chop down at Marek's neck. The madman fell forward stunned, tried to get up and then collapsed face down on the deck.

The ship's siren was shrieking.

'Air escaping! Air escaping! Hull damaged in section fifteen.'

Jerry tried to take in a deep breath of air, but there was no air left to breathe. He staggered towards the control console.

'Order to Ship,' he gasped. 'Order to Ship – instant emergency sealing procedure.'

'Order received.'

Cathy held the laser-gun limply, leaning against the panel. The laser ray had burned a hole in the hull and that was why the air was escaping. Normally the ship would have acted automatically to reseal the hole, but evidently Marek's repairs to the cybernetic system had not been wholly successful.

Within seconds the siren had stopped and the ship's brain reported: 'Air pressure returning to normal. Hull section temporarily repaired.'

Between the two layers of titanium making up the ship's outer hull was a viscous pseudo-metallic substance that could be released to 'plug' any small hole that might appear in the hull.

'Begin permanent repair operation,' Jerry told the ship as he checked the instruments and gratefully breathed in the fresh supply of oxygen pumped into the cabin from the hydroponics section.

He switched to a view on the television screen of the outside of the hull at section fifteen. Within moments a small repair robot had left its special 'kennel' in the outer hull and was crawling along towards the damaged area, its bright metal body glinting in the dazzling light of Alpha Centauri.

The little robot was soon busy 'patching' the hull with a plate of titanium and Jerry returned his attention to Marek's prone body.

'We'd better restrain him in some way, I suppose,' he said to Catherine.

She shrugged. 'I suppose so. What shall we do – tie him up?'

They had not anticipated violence and thus were in no way prepared to deal with the problem that Marek now presented.

'Don't forget, Jerry,' Catherine said in a low voice. 'We're still heading towards Alpha Centauri at far too great a speed for safety.'

Jerry had forgotten in the excitement. He knew it was too risky to decelerate suddenly, particularly with the hull weakened by the laser beam.

And yet – they *were* dangerously close to the nearest of the flaming orange spheres.

'We'll just have to slow down as rapidly as we dare,' he said, 'and slightly alter course at the same time.'

He gave the necessary orders to the ship and then they picked up Marek and carried him back to the crew quarters. Catherine rolled up his sleeve and administered a strong sedative and then they lashed him to his bunk as best they could, returning speedily to the Control Room to check their speed and direction.

They were still travelling too fast. The huge, alien sun had grown to an enormous size in the main observation port. It blinded them.

Grimly Jerry closed the port. 'It's the sun's gravity,' he said. 'It's pulling us towards it! Unless we think of something quickly, we're going to be drawn into the heart of the star and be vaporised in seconds!'

Catherine was checking the ship's co-ordinates.

'We'll just have to turn her completely round,' She said. 'Head back into deep space. Damn Marek. If he hadn't

distracted us, we'd have anticipated all this. As it was, we emerged into ordinary space far closer to Alpha Centauri than we'd originally planned.'

'It's a question of fuel, too,' Jerry reminded her. 'If we start moving away from the sun now, it will take an enormous amount of our fuel – and maybe leave us without enough to do what we came here to do.'

'Perhaps even strand us here,' Catherine agreed. She lifted her head. 'Order to Ship. Please scan all areas of space in the immediate vicinity. Use all screens.'

'Order received.'

Now they looked at areas of space away from the suns, desperately searching for signs of planets – planets where the ship might land and convert chemicals into fuel for the atomic pile that was the ship's source of power.

Suddenly Catherine pointed. 'Look! Look at that Jerry!'

A planet had appeared on one of the screens. It was a large planet – about the size of Jupiter. A planet of bright, pale blue and white.

'Hold view on Screen Eight,' Jerry commanded the ship. 'Alter course for planetary body in view.'

'Order received.'

Now, as the ship obeyed the order, the blue planet grew larger on the screen. It was so much bigger than Earth that it was plain that the gravity must be considerably greater and that it would not be a habitable world for human beings, even if it was capable in other respects of supporting human life.

But it *was* a planet and, if the worst came to the worst, they could always land the ship on it and send out robots to find the necessary chemicals to process for their fuel supply.

But now, as the ship approached the blue planet, they saw that it possessed several moons. And the moons themselves were larger than Earth!

Jerry pointed at a reddish coloured moon circling the planet. 'That might be better to land on. The gravity would probably be about right. Order to Ship, close in on moon on Screen Five. Prepare to make preliminary survey.'

'Order received.'

Now the ship altered course slightly and headed for the red moon. Gradually they began to make out details. The redness seemed to come from a thick cloud layer. Soon the ship began to chant out the results of its preliminary checks.

'Gravity 1.7 Earth's. Atmosphere contains only minimum percentage oxygen – predominately ammonia. Cannot support human life. Repeat, cannot support human life.'

'I hadn't expected it to,' grinned Jerry. The ship was principally programmed to discover Earth-type worlds. 'Order to Ship – give me a complete breakdown of gases near the surface of the world, please.'

The ship began to chant out the component gases of the moon's atmosphere.

Jerry frowned. 'Doesn't sound too hopeful. It would take a long while to process that lot and I'm still worried about the weakened hull.'

'Ship to commander – ship to commander. Reporting smaller body in view.'

Now they could see it on the screen. A moon orbiting the red moon!

'Moons on moons!' Cathy smiled. 'We're certainly getting a lot to choose from!'

The moon orbiting the red moon was about two-thirds the size of Earth and seemed to be rotating pretty rapidly on its own axis while it encircled its parent moon.

'Scientists predicted the possibility of moons being large enough to have moons encircling them,' Jerry said in astonishment, 'but I never expected to see something like it!'

'Gravity approximately .8 Earth's. Atmosphere primarily oxygen. Rotation approximately 18 hours. Orbit approximately 9 months. Can support human life. Repeat – *can support human life!*'

Jerry was unable to speak. He stared at Catherine and she stared back.

This is what they had come to Alpha Centauri to find. A world that could support human life. A new world – an unspoiled world. A world where people equipped with all the knowledge and science of the twenty-first century could begin afresh!

'Cathy!' Jerry murmured at last. 'We've found it – we've found New Earth. And we found it almost by accident!'

He hugged his wife tightly and he was weeping with relief. All the strains of the voyage had been worthwhile.

'Ship to commander. Ship to commander. Fuel reserve dangerously low. Advise landing on Earth-type world. Advise landing on Earth-type world.'

Jerry nodded. He put his arm around Cathy's shoulders. 'Well, Cathy – this is it. Are you ready?'

She smiled her agreement.

'Order to Ship,' said Jerry softly. 'Prepare to make landing on Earth-type world.'

'Order received.'

They watched as the world came closer and closer.

The ship's instruments danced and clicked.

The world they approached was not the predominantly blue-green of Earth, but reflected the reddish light of the moon around which it circled. As they approached it they saw that there were clouds and below the clouds were what appeared to be large land areas and smaller areas of water. The land areas seemed chiefly coloured a kind of reddish-yellow.

Now they strapped themselves into their couches. The ship was ready to decelerate and circle the world on the fringes of its upper atmosphere in order for the crew to make preliminary surveys before landing.

As the ship slowed, Jerry felt the familiar sickening sensation. He grew dizzy, blacked out momentarily, and then it was over. The ship was circling the world, like some infinitely smaller moon.

Unstrapping himself from the couch, Jerry gave the ship orders to show the world's continents at close range.

Mountains and valleys appeared. Rivers and plains. Forests and lakes. All had a peculiarly *alien* quality, hard to define, though they were quite similar, at this range, to those on Earth.

They moved rapidly. Whole continents came and went. Jerry ordered the ship to decrease its speed even further. Now the planet below them passed less swiftly by. They were over an area that seemed to be a plateau similar to the Matto Grosso region on Earth, though covered with orange vegetation. It looked an ideal place for landing.

'I think we'll make planet-fall here,' Jerry said to Catherine, turning his head to address his wife. 'What do you think?'

'Seems fine,' she agreed. 'I'll – Good God! Jerry – look at that! Look at it Jerry, quickly, before we pass it!'

Jerry stared at the screen unable to believe his eyes.

He was looking at a city. A strange, ancient city that also looked somehow modern.

Then it was gone.

Jerry looked at his wife, unable to voice the thought that was in both their minds.

It seemed that New Earth was already inhabited. And it was too late to change their minds about landing. Already the ship was speaking.

'Preparing to land. Preparing to land.'

Jerry let the ship continue with its landing procedures. There was nothing else to do. He could only hope that the inhabitants of this world were not hostile. His lips were dry as the ship began to descend towards the strange, orange plain.

CHAPTER NINE

The Hope of Man slid downwards through the thickening atmosphere of the strange satellite world – a world almost as large as Earth, yet dwarfed by the red planet about which it spun.

Flecks of orange cloud dappled the continents that sprawled beneath the spaceship and the sky turned rapidly from black to violet to blue.

A high, thin screaming filled the Control Room as the ship's listening devices transmitted the rush of heated gases across the outer hull.

Jerry Cornelius, staring at the massed banks of television screens above the instrument panels, licked his dry lips as he mentally pictured the slender tongue of fire that blazed from the rear propulsion tubes, the fire that supported thousands of tons of steel, plastics and titanium against the monstrous pull of the satellite's gravity.

He was helpless now. The brain of the ship was in full control of the landing procedure. He thought of Frank Marek's rage-distorted face and of the damage that the brain had suffered during their horrifying passage through hyperspace. Marek had repaired the brain, or so he claimed, and Cathy and Jerry had believed him.

But now Marek himself was unbalanced, a victim of the same forces that had overcome the ship. How long

49

had he been affected before his attempt to kill his two companions?

'Jerry – is something wrong?'

He glanced up sharply and saw his wife's eyes gazing at him intently. Her pale face reflected some of his own tenseness. Jerry smiled, briefly.

'Sorry, darling. That business with Frank must have shaken me more than I realised. Blood and thunder isn't my line.'

The voice of the ship broke in before she could reply. *'Stand by for landing! Three minutes to touchdown! Please secure your safety-webbing.'*

At the touch of a switch, the pilot's chairs lowered and extended themselves, becoming padded couches capable of cushioning their occupants against bumps or vibration, while a flexible web of rubbery strands closed about them like a folding flower.

Above Jerry's upturned face the landscape of the alien world expanded – flowing outwards to the borders of the television screens as the ship rushed stern-first towards the landing point. A storm of radiations and sonic pulses beat upon the earth below. They came from her complex instruments, probing, assessing the nature of the air, the soil and vegetation, the rock strata upon which the weight of the giant craft would rest.

Jerry's last, wry thought before ship and planet met was that it was fortunate they were not hoping to land unobserved; the people of the mysterious city glimpsed during their approach would scarcely be dull-witted enough to have missed their fiery, thunderous descent.

And then they were down.

The Hope of Man shuddered, settled a little and was still.

Into the numbing silence that followed the shut-down of the engines crept a myriad lesser sounds. The groan and creak of cooling metal, the whirr of countless mechanical devices, and the faint crackling of burning vegetation borne to them through the sound pick-ups outside. Thick, purplish smoke drifted across the viewfield of the television scanners, shot through with rays of orange sunlight.

'Commander to ship,' said Jerry quietly. 'Kill those fires. I want no smoke.' He turned to Cathy. 'If there are inhabitants in that city, I want to find them before they find us. They might be hostile. The ship's conspicuous enough without adding smoke-signals.'

Cathy undid the web. 'Please, Jerry – don't be such a pessimist.' She slid lithely from her couch. 'Why should they want to harm us? What possible threat could we be to an entire world?'

Jerry rose, laughing. 'That's my girl! Back on Earth they're ready to blow each other apart for the sake of a line on a map! Can you imagine how suspicious a lot of Earth people would be of an alien planet landing there? But you could be right. I hope so.'

Cathy frowned slightly. 'I'd better take a look at Frank. The sedative ought to be wearing off by now.'

Jerry followed her along the narrow corridor to the living quarters. As the door slid aside and they stepped into the compact, cheerful room, he heard a voice muttering thickly. It was hardly recognisable as that of Frank Marek. Even though no words were distinguishable, the note of terror in the voice was clear.

Cathy hurried to the bunk where he lay, tied securely by Jerry, and quickly checked his pulse and temperature. He moved restlessly, straining against the tough cords, breathing harshly.

'How is he?'

Cathy spoke slowly. 'Physically, he's fine. His pulse-rate's a little fast, but otherwise . . .' She paused. 'Jerry, what can we do for him if his mind is still affected when he wakes?'

Jerry ran a hand over his thick blond hair. 'The Lord only knows.' He looked down at Marek's agitated face, bent over him, his mouth close to Marek's ear. 'Frank. Frank, can you hear me?'

Marek stiffened. Then, very suddenly, his body relaxed, sagging in his bonds. He drew one great, gasping breath and then his eyelids fluttered open and he stared straight into Jerry's eyes. A smile curved on his broad mouth.

51

'Hello, Jerry. That third jump was a rough one, eh? I guess I must be getting old. How close are we to Centauri?'

Cathy, standing at the head of the bunk just out of range of Marek's vision, flashed a warning glance at Jerry and mouthed silently: 'Amnesia.'

'Pretty rough, Frank,' said Jerry, with genuine relief. 'You took a nasty tumble just as we went into hyperspace. Sorry we had to tie you down, but you were threshing around quite a lot.' He grinned. 'I have bruises to prove it.'

Marek became aware of the restraining cords for the first time. 'Oh. A hell of a situation for an old spaceman! I'll never live this down if the Astronaut's Club gets to hear of it.' Abruptly his tone sharpened. 'The engines have stopped. Are we in trouble?'

'No, Frank.' Cathy came to his side as Jerry began to untie him. 'Frank – we're down. We've landed upon an inhabitable world. Air and water and vegetation – and there may be other Earth-type worlds in this system!'

'Bullseye with the first shot, eh?' Marek grunted. He sat up, massaging his wrists, flexing his leg muscles. 'Well, let's go and see what we've found. You haven't been outside yet, have you?'

'Not yet.' Cathy sounded slightly piqued by his matter-of-fact reaction.

'We fired a few acres of grass, or whatever it is, when we touched down,' explained Jerry. 'I had the chemical-foam sprays turned on to smother the smoke and flames. Everything should be clear shortly.'

'But there's more than that, Frank,' Cathy declared. *'We saw a city!'*

'A city? You're certain?' Marek swung down from the bunk. He straightened and then swayed. Jerry caught his arm, steadying him. The older man shook his head irritably. 'I'm all right. Just stiff, that's all. Lead on.'

Blackened earth and rapidly-drying patches of white foam surrounded the ship. At the limit of the scanner's range a faint orange haze blurred the horizon. Under a vivid blue sky the land lay empty and inviting. Jerry gave a last glance at the screens and said briskly, 'According to the ship's analyses of soil and atmosphere everything out there looks good. So let's get started.'

A short while later, clad now in the grey, silk-smooth coveralls designed for outdoor work, the trio stood in the airlock chamber, blinking in the glare of an alien sun. The air flooding into their lungs still carried the bitter smell of burnt vegetation, but a rich medley of scents underlay this. Already a feeling of exhilaration stirred the travellers, wiping out the memories of their recent troubles. Squatting far below them on the ashes was a sturdy six-wheeled vehicle, unloaded automatically from the ship's cargo compartment at Jerry's command. Light, powerful and capacious, it was the latest product of a long line of incredibly rugged carriers that had evolved during the wars of the twentieth century. Between the airlock and the carrier stretched a telescopic stairway of silvery metal. Marek gestured to it.

'Commander?'

'Without you, Frank, we'd probably still be wandering in hyperspace,' Jerry smiled. 'Yours should be the first foot to touch ground.'

Marek grunted. 'It strikes me,' he said, 'that we're both being unforgivably rude to a lady. After you my dear.'

Cathy did not hesitate. The two men followed her down the stairway.

Still thirty feet from the ground, Marek gasped. Jerry looked back as the older man faltered, then fell. Only Jerry's lightning-fast reflexes prevented him from being hurled headlong by the impact of the scientist's stocky body. With straining muscles he clung to the handrail. The dead weight of Marek dragging at his left arm, he gave an involuntary cry. Cathy turned. Now she sprang to his aid. Together they carried the inert body into the ship.

They did not leave *The Hope of Man* again that day.

Late in the evening Marek had recovered consciousness and seemed none the worse for his experience. But he agreed with Jerry when the latter suggested, on Cathy's advice, that he should remain with the ship while his younger companions carried out the preliminary survey of their new world. It had been a tiring day, but Jerry did not sleep well.

CHAPTER TEN

At a distance of three miles, the gleaming hull was still an impressive sight, towering up from a tangle of blue-green foliage. The carrier's sextuple wheels hissed along over dark, mossy growths still wet with the overnight rain and a cool breeze fluttered Cathy's auburn hair. With Jerry at the wheel they had made good time since leaving the ship, moving across a level plateau that invited speed.

Forests marched to right and left – strange bulbous 'trees' that reminded them of the ancient pillars of Minoan palaces, crowned with fountain-like bursts of slender leaves, and a dense undergrowth of violet, blue and sepia stalks flowering about their roots.

The land that had seemed so empty on the television screens actually swarmed with life. Shining insect-like things as big as jackrabbits fled before their advance, leaping with dream-like power on this low-gravity planet. Through the cloud-flecked sky moved creatures of breathtaking size, translucent and tenuous, trailing iridescent whiplike cilia. Cathy manipulated camera and sound recorder almost continuously, until Jerry accused her of being an interstellar tourist. She dug an elbow into his ribs in reply, and he fended her off with one hand, laughing.

In the middle of this mock struggle the carrier dipped into a shallow valley and executed a spectacular skid before Jerry regained full control of the wheel. They rocked to a halt and fell against each other in helpless mirth.

Thunder bellowed in the distance and was flung back from the far hills. It built up and up, a long crescendo of sound that could have only one source.

White-faced, Cathy stared at her husband. 'My God, Jerry – *it's the ship!*'

Jerry had the carrier in motion already, the engine snarling as they raced up the slope. But even as they shot over the crest, a blinding pillar of fire leapt into the sky from the landing-site, higher and yet higher, becoming a bright point against the blue, an after-image on the eye and then – nothing.

Stunned, they sat there until the thunder died into silence.

'Could it have been an accident, Jerry?'

Jerry stirred, looked at her. 'It could be. The ship's brain was never fully repaired . . . Damn it, Cathy, we both know that take-off wasn't an accident! Frank's up there now in full charge with his mind full of God knows what twisted ideas!'

'And now?'

He thumbed the engine into life, swung the carrier's blunt nose about to face the hazy horizon.

'The city, Cathy. Where else?'

Towards the close of the planet's short day, with their elongated shadow rippling over the plain before them they had their second view of the city.

The huge red primary of their satellite world had risen ponderously above the hills, fringing the plateau – a sullen, mottled ball suspended in the darkening sky, and beneath it the weird cluster of towers and domes crouched in the shadow.

Despite the warmth of her heated suit, Cathy shivered.

'It looks like a colossal cemetery. I'd almost prefer to spend the night in the carrier.'

'Me, too,' said Jerry. 'If there were any lights over there they ought to be visible from here, but I can't see a glimmer.'

The city seemed dead.

Then Jerry blinked, rubbing his eyes, craning his neck. He thought he had seen a flash of brightness – something . . .

He raised binoculars to his eyes. And then he saw it!

From out of the city walls came something great and glittering. A mechanism of metal and crystal that floated through the purple dusk. Dying sunlight caught facets of its complex surfaces as it turned, so that its shape fluctuated and never seemed the same from moment to moment.

'My God! An aircraft of some kind!'

Jerry reached for the curved stock of the laser rifle clipped to the carrier's side, placed the weapon in its swivel mounting at shoulder level.

The glittering machine came on.

A figure sat within it.

The glittering machine was even closer now, but Jerry couldn't get a strong impression of the figure occupying it. His hand gripped the stock of the laser rifle and he noted abstractedly that there was sweat on it.

Was the occupant of the flying machine human? Again this was difficult to judge.

Cathy put a hand on Jerry's shoulder. 'Jerry – shouldn't we – shouldn't we make for cover or something?'

'Don't worry, Cathy – this laser rifle gives us plenty of protection should we need it. I'm counting on the fact that whoever it is in that aircraft is as curious about us as we are about them . . .'

The machine came to a halt about a hundred yards from

their carrier and hovered in the twilight air, its crystal and metal body still catching some of the fading sunlight. Above it dark orange clouds crossed the sky. Somewhere a strange, unearthly cry sounded.

Now the machine began to descend to the reddish-yellow plain and landed.

Jerry and Cathy waited tensely.

Nothing happened for a moment.

Then there was a whine and part of the machine's canopy slid back. From the opening the figure emerged.

'It's a biped, at least,' said Jerry.

The biped was tall and thin – about seven feet tall. It left the machine and with long, graceful movements came towards the carrier. It seemed clad in some sort of highly flexible metal cloth, with a mask covering its entire face.

Jerry's pulse-rate increased. He wiped the sweat from his left hand on his overalls.

About five yards from them the figure stopped and raised one thin, metal-clad arm. A sonorous, echoing voice came from the helmet.

'*Yoasha, hana, canala . . .*'

Jerry shook his head, trying to indicate that he did not understand.

'*Yoasha, hana, canala . . .*' The voice seemed more insistent this time.

Again Jerry tried to show that he did not know what the creature was saying.

'*Yoasha, hana, canala – TEY!*'

The figure turned and pointed at his aircraft.

'He wants us to get in it,' Cathy said. 'Oh, Jerry – I wish . . .'

Jerry tightened his grip on the gun. 'I'll compromise, I think.' With gestures he tried to tell the creature that he would follow the aircraft back to the city in the carrier. You go – we follow.

The alien seemed to deliberate for a moment and then was apparently satisfied. He raised an arm.

'*Yoasha kompla.*'

He returned to his aircraft and it took off, flying only a few feet from the ground, Jerry started up the carrier and began to follow.

Now it was almost dark, but the outlines of the strange city could still be seen against the horizon. Jerry switched on the carrier's headlights.

'I hope they're friendly, Jerry,' said Cathy with a little shudder.

'So do I. My God, they'd better be. Without the spaceship, we're stranded here forever.'

'Why do you think Frank took off again?'

'Who's to say. His mind is unbalanced. He might even have forgotten we were down here. Maybe he plans to return . . .'

'The ship's already short of fuel. He never refuelled. He hasn't a chance of getting back to Earth. No-one will ever know what became of us – or *The Hope of Man.*'

'They'll send another ship out sooner or later,' Jerry reassured her.

'But *will* they? You know how bad conditions were getting on Earth. It may be too late. War is bound to break out soon if we don't get back and tell them that there are planets out here that can be colonised.'

Jerry could not reply to this. She was right. Unless a miracle happened, *The Hope of Man* was the last spaceship to leave Earth before the final cataclysm overwhelmed her.

CHAPTER ELEVEN

They were close to the city. And now it had taken on a menacing air. Its towers were huge, assymetrical structures that seemed to have been built by madmen. There was something unnatural about every line of the architecture, every choice of colour or carving. And yet there was also a sense of great strength about it, of purpose and intelligence.

'Surely the people who built this are not human beings,' Cathy murmured. 'It really is – *alien*.'

Jerry nodded. The crystal machine had reached the wall, a section of which was opening to admit it. He followed it through.

Strange smells, a peculiar mood.

They followed the machine through twisting, narrow streets, the towers rising high above them, threatening and gloomy.

Now at last the crystal machine stopped and the tall, thin alien got out, signalling for them to follow. Jerry took the laser rifle off its rest and handed another gun to Cathy. 'Stay ready for trouble,' he said.

The city was only illuminated by the light from the stars.

Jerry got out of the carrier and trod a surface very much like black marble, walking cautiously towards the alien, Cathy following immediately behind.

61

The alien entered a dark entrance of the nearest tower. Jerry took a deep breath and followed.

A faint luminescence filled the interior of the tower as they walked along a narrow passage and entered a hall with a surprisingly low ceiling – barely eight feet from the floor.

'Ugh!' Cathy sniffed. 'The smell – it's horrid!'

'It is pretty strong,' Jerry admitted. 'Strange – all this sophisticated science and yet apparently no decent sanitation . . .'

Now the alien led them through a series of narrow corridors until it came to another chamber in which a thin light glowed, illuminating a series of barbaric murals which, though abstract, were subtly horrifying.

Cathy glanced away 'There's something very wrong about this place. It isn't just that it's an alien city – it somehow doesn't seem to be functioning in the way it was originally designed.'

'I know what you mean.' Jerry studied the murals. 'Maybe . . .'

'*Yoasha chanda!*' The sonorous voice echoed and boomed. '*Yoasha chanda!*' The figure came to a dead stop and remained where it was without a muscle moving.

The air was full of tension as Jerry and Cathy waited for it to speak again or give them some signal. Minutes passed. Jerry checked his chronometer impatiently. The minutes became a quarter of an hour.

At length Jerry approached the figure. 'What's happening? What are you playing at?'

There was no response.

He went around the alien and faced him. 'What's going on, friend?'

Still no response.

The figure was completely immobile.

Jerry reached out to touch him. The alien made no effort to stop him. He touched dead, cold metal that sent a chill through his entire body. He pushed the alien against the chest. It rocked but otherwise made no movement.

'Is he – has he died, Jerry?' Cathy murmured.

Jerry frowned. 'I'm not sure. Perhaps he isn't . . .' He reached up to touch the head. It was not a mask that the creature was wearing at all. The featureless helmet *was* its head. Jerry moved his hand down the alien's chest until his hand touched a small oval panel set in the metal. With a fingernail he pulled at the panel. At last it swung out, revealing a set of controls of a bizarre design.

'A robot!' Cathy gasped. 'It isn't a living creature at all! A metal man!'

Jerry nodded. 'That means we have still to meet the true inhabitants of the city – presuming they exist.'

'But why did the robot stop?'

'It's hard to say. Perhaps it was programmed to greet visitors and bring them to this part of the city. Perhaps its masters are away or dead or something, but it followed its original program, bringing us here where, under normal circumstances, we would have been met by the people – or creatures – who live here. They are probably quite like us in appearance.'

'How do you know that, Jerry?'

'Because the robot is fashioned in the form of a man. Why else would they design it in this way? Not the most practical design for a robot, you must admit!'

Cathy smiled. 'I suppose you're right. What do we do now?'

'We explore. It's a good opportunity to take a look around while the inhabitants are away – if away they are.'

'But why would they leave an entire city uninhabited?'

'Who's to explain the workings of an alien mind?'

'Perhaps something drove them from the city,' Cathy suggested. 'Something terrifying – that might still be here!'

'We'll have to risk that. We've no choice. We're here now, after all.' Jerry gave her a reassuring smile. 'Come on, Cathy.'

They entered another tunnel and moved cautiously along it until, at length, they emerged into the air again. They were in an open courtyard formed by the inner walls of the tower. There were a number of entrances on every side of the courtyard. In the middle of the courtyard was a fountain. Jerry moved towards it and inspected it as best he could in the darkness.

'The water's dried up. It doesn't look as if it's been used for years. You're right, Cathy – the city does seem permanently deserted, and yet . . .' He frowned. 'Don't you get the sense that it *is* inhabited? I do.'

'I know what you mean,' nodded his wife. 'Ugh – this place gives me the shakes. Let's get back to our carrier, Jerry.'

'Okay.'

They made their way back through the corridors, past the immobile robot, along through the other passages until they came back to the entrance to the tower, the street and their carrier.

It was Cathy who noticed it first. 'The aircraft, Jerry – it's gone.'

It was true. The crystal flying machine was no longer there.

'Perhaps it returned automatically to wherever it came from,' Jerry suggested.

Cathy shivered and climbed into the carrier. Then she shouted again.

'Jerry! Your binoculars. They've disappeared. Someone – or something – has taken them.'

'Oh, they're probably just . . .' Jerry began to walk towards the carrier and then stopped.

From somewhere behind him had come a stealthy sound. A scuttling sound. A slithering sound. He wheeled round.

There was a giggle – high-pitched, insane. Jerry flicked the safety catch off the laser rifle.

'What's out there? Who are you?'

Again the giggle. Again the slithering sound. Jerry saw something moving in the shadows and he aimed his gun high, sending a beam of pure energy into the sky.

By its light he made out the shape.

If these were the inhabitants, then they had *not* made the robot in their own form.

Jerry gasped in horror!

Crouched in the seat of the carrier Cathy stared at people of

the city and panic swelled within her. She fought it down – forced her mind to accept what she saw.

They were human in shape – clearly, sickeningly human. Jerry, silhouetted against the blinding glare of the laser rifle, towered over a semi-circle of grotesque figures. Frozen in attitudes of shock by the sudden burst of light, the dark mass of their hunched bodies and their white, blank-eyed faces formed a nightmare tableau. In that first vivid glimpse Cathy could not distinguish between male and female, young and old. Their clothes were rags and tatters, smeared with a hundred hues in bizarre and gloomy patchwork. Around the necks of some, on cords, hung objects that quivered and glittered.

Without turning Jerry said quietly: 'Put the spotlight on them, Cathy. But don't make any sudden movements.'

The sound of his voice seemed to release her from a spell. Rising slowly she stepped into the rear section of the carrier. Unmasking the spotlight, she swung it smoothly about and clicked it into life. At the same moment, Jerry released the laser's trigger. Darkness rushed in around them. Across the spotlight's pale beam fell silver streaks of rain. The huddled group stirred suddenly, shuffling forward.

'Jerry – please get into the carrier!' Shadows danced across the tower walls as the spotlight responded to the tensing of Cathy's muscles.

'Steady, darling – relax.' Jerry smiled grimly. 'Remember I have the laser rifle and none of this bunch seems to be armed. I'm going to try to talk to them.'

He drew a deep breath, swallowing hard as the acrid stench of the strangers filled his nostrils. Then, mimicking the tones of the robot guide as nearly as he could, he cried: 'Yoasha chanda!'

The group halted.

A rapid gabbling broke out among them. Their heads bobbed, their hands moved in a disorganised way, rubbing and plucking at their garments. The rain increased, spattering on the black streets, rattling on the carrier's metal sides. Jerry waited in mingled wariness and despair. Who were these creatures? Had *they* built this massive and complex city, and if so, what had destroyed their humanity?

Cathy screamed.

He whirled, swinging the laser at hip level. A swarm of figures, like tattered apes, were pouring from the low doorway of a nearby tower. Two had already reached the carrier and were climbing aboard. The spotlight swivelled crazily as Cathy sprang aside from their clutching fingers. Jerry vaulted into the vehicle hearing a sudden wild uproar behind him.

'Start her up!' he yelled. 'I'll hold them off!'

He plunged forward. Slavering and spitting, two creatures flung themselves in his path. Reluctant even now to use the laser beam upon them he slammed the rifle-butt at the side of one man's head, dropped the other with a blow to the chest. A hand grabbed at his ankle. He fell, painfully, against the spotlight and rolled away from the swinging, flat-handed blows of his attackers. They were coming from both sides now, filling the night with an insane and toneless howling. Cathy felt an arm lock about her throat, dragging her head backwards. Gagging, she fought to start the engine, bracing her body against the pull. As the carrier jerked forward, she heard a thud and the choking pressure ceased. A body slithered from the carrier's side into the rain-slashed roadway. Jerry fell into the seat beside her, panting, shaking one raw-knuckled hand. They roared into a glassy wall of rain, wheels throwing up sheets of spray to either side. He jabbed a button and the windscreen extended itself to become a transparent canopy of tough plastic. The sound of shouting faded behind them, swallowed by the drumbeat of falling water. Cathy called above the din: 'Are you hurt?'

'Scraped knuckles,' he said. 'Nothing more. Are you okay?'

A huge pillar loomed out of the rain, squarely in their path. Jerry made a futile, instinctive braking motion and then was thrown sideways as the carrier swerved. Cathy spun the wheel, feeling the vehicle swing wide under the weaker gravity. The headlights flared across twisting stairways, crazily angled walls, dark arches, an open gateway. They shot between jagged metallic columns into a dimly-seen square. The carrier slowed, braked. Cathy fell back against the padded headrest, smiling wanly.

'I'm okay, thanks. But I can't take any more of this maniac's maze. Where are we going?'

Jerry laughed shortly. 'I should know? Move over, darling – I'll take the wheel. What we need is to find an exit from this place without running into our little friends again. There must be more than one gateway in the city walls.'

He eased the carrier forward and put the spotlight on remote control, sweeping the beam to and fro automatically. It seemed to penetrate the downpour only slightly more than did the headlamps.

'Try the detectors,' Cathy suggested.

'Good idea – they may be of use now that we have space to manoeuvre.'

Jerry activated the twin telescopic antennae behind the canopy, and as an afterthought switched on the radio. On the carrier's console, a small screen began to glow, building up a ghostly image of their surroundings as the antennae pulsed signals into the night. Thunder banged somewhere overhead. The radio crackled. Cathy drew out a pocket mirror and grimaced at the disarray of her hair.

'Jerry, do you think we'll find anyone else in the city? Anyone – sane?'

He drove slowly, peering at the screen. 'We certainly made a wonderful first contact back there, didn't we? A true meeting of minds . . .' His tone was light, but she sensed the worry behind his words. 'No, Cathy, I can't see any hope of discovering intelligent life here. Did you recognise the objects those people were wearing around their necks?'

'No,' she answered, faintly puzzled. 'I didn't get a close look at them.'

'I did! Those baubles were scientific instruments, Cathy – scientific instruments! Beautifully finished, too, so far as I could tell!'

A profound depression settled over her as the implications of his statement sank home.

'Then we're lost. Frank has marooned us on a world filled with – with – Morlocks!'

'Eh?' said Jerry, darting a glance at her. 'Filled with *what*?'

'Morlocks,' Cathy repeated. 'They were characters in a 19th century novel. They looked like apes and operated vast machines in caves beneath the earth.'

He grunted. 'I doubt if our bunch were capable of running a clockwork train, let alone vast machines. Their clumsiness was the only thing that saved us.'

She pointed at the screen. 'Look!'

Shadowy green shapes filled the viewfield, a luminous barrier of spires, domes and arches, an architectural cliff. The distance indicator told Jerry that the reality lay slightly more than a mile ahead. He accelerated slightly: 'Taking to the high ground is a good old military maxim when in doubt. That central archway looks as if it has an ascending ramp leading off from it. Maybe we can reach a level from which we can see a way to the walls.'

On the screen, a rectangular blur detached itself from the background. It expanded as they watched. Abruptly it quivered, seemed momentarily to divide, and rippled into shapelessness. The radio emitted a deafening barrage of squeals and growls, mixed with a curious thudding like the beat of a giant heart.

'Whatever *that* was, it was big!' Jerry snapped. 'And it was heading our way. I don't like the way it blanked out our detectors. Better get the laser rifle mounted, Cathy.'

'The image split,' she said. 'There could be two of them.'

'Then let's not hang around!' He sent the carrier surging

forward, water cascading from its sleek sides. Cathy slid from the front seat into the retractable turret that served to hold telescope or gun. Deftly she fitted the laser into its mounting. The rain slammed against the plastic cupola in slanting white rods and the world was a glistening darkness. The rifle barrel jutting from the watertight iris of the turret seemed a feeble threat to the forces raging in the night.

Blue-green lightning flamed through the lowering clouds, illuminating the square with theatrical vividness. Crests of towers and curves of domes gleamed ahead. Jerry caught his breath as a monstrous bulk moved into view to their left, parting the curtains of rain with a metallic prow. Thunder broke like an avalanche as the light blinked out. He gripped the wheel with aching hands and drove straight for the unseen distant doorway. The screen was useless now, a rectangle of flickering grey-green.

'Jerry! To your left!'

He jerked his head around as the laser blazed. Towering high above him rose a mass of metal, a whirling nightmare of blades and wheels from which waterfalls poured. Cursing, he spun the wheel, canting the carrier to the limits of its stability in a screeching turn. Something smashed into the stones of the square behind him and he felt the shock vibrate throughout the chassis.

Splinters clanged from the bodywork, rattled on the cupola. Cathy swung the bright flame of the laser, seeking a vital spot in the chaotic jumble of shape and shadow. A great arm, spiked with metre-long blades, swept across the canopy.

Jerry flinched. Glass shattered. Metal screeched.

And the spotlight went out.

The carrier bounced.

He was still fighting to control it when a pair of toothed jaws settled upon the canopy and bit into the steel-hard plastic.

The front wheels lost traction, spinning helplessly as the claw began to raise the vehicle clear of the ground.

'I can't stop it, Jerry! The laser doesn't do anything to it!' White-faced, Cathy hung onto the rifle's butt, slashing with futile strokes of concentrated light at the armoured monster.

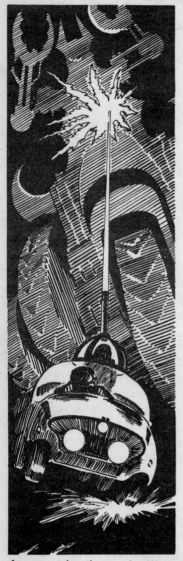

Cursing, Jerry reached for a red toggle-switch set into a recess in the console. 'Get down!' he yelled. 'I'm going to blow the canopy!'

She dropped into a crouch, arms wrapped about her head. He yanked the switch, and flung himself face-down upon the driving seat. A split-second later, the emergency release mechanism detonated the explosive bolts set around the cabin's perimeter. The canopy ruptured and bulged. The jaws of the grab clashed together as resistance vanished, and a violent thrust pushed the carrier earthwards. Dazed and deafened, Jerry groped for the controls.

Scarcely knowing what he was doing, he sent the vehicle rocketing forward. Before they had gone a hundred yards, the interior was awash, but they were not aware of the rain.

Somewhere ahead was refuge, and their minds had room for nothing else at that moment. The doorway was already visible in the headlamp beams.

Then, from the murk behind them, a titanic crash, like the meeting of worlds, shivered through the air. They looked at each other wide-eyed.

Cathy said:

'The second machine?'

Jerry's answering grin was close to a snarl. 'It sounds as if it met the first one!'

Then they began to laugh, and the laughter became wild and hysterical till Cathy passed into tears. The carrier took the ramp easily, bearing them up into a vaulted interior where luminescent panels threw a cold, dim light at intervals along the way. Elaborate galleries and arcades wandered off into stygian gloom. Exterior noises faded, and the purr of the engine echoed back from unguessable depths and hollows of stone.

It was strangely soothing, and so they were lulled and unready when the final attack came.

'It's like an artificial mountain,' whispered Cathy, now somewhat recovered. 'Why would people want to shut themselves inside such a mass of stone?'

'Lord knows.' Jerry's voice, too, was subdued. 'Fear of the outer world, maybe?' He shook his head. 'I'm no psychologist.'

He was about to move off from the intersection of ramp and gallery where they were parked, when a mass of dark figures erupted from a side tunnel only yards away. There was no time to escape, no space to use the gun. They went down under a squirming clawing tangle of bodies, choking on the sour stench of dirt and sweat. Jerry fought with scientific savagery and the superior strength of Earthly muscles, developed under a gravity-pull greater than anything known on this lighter world. He rose clear of the struggle for a moment, and had a strange, fleeting impression that the robot-guide they had encountered outside the city was standing some distance away, aloof and watching. It was his last clear thought for some time. Lights pierced the shadows, irregular, flickering lights of many colours that swiftly established a compelling rhythm. His opponents fell away from him, and lay huddled and inert. Thoughts leaped into his mind in wild disorder. A street in London he had known . . . years ago . . . pillared porticoes . . . busy traffic. Then the scene darkened. There were craters, snow, a sea of mud. Cathy and Frank were there; he spoke to them and they answered and yet he knew somehow they were dead. And then it all faded, down, down into blackness and oblivion.

He woke. A girl in a short, silvery tunic leaned over him. She was small, pretty, hazel-eyed. Blonde hair framed her unsmiling face. As Jerry's eyes came fully open, her expression brightened. She said:

'My name is Lae-Pinu. Who are you?'

Jerry stared at her, speechless. She was speaking English – clear, fluent English! He tried to rise, but something held his head down. He reached up, and felt a cold metallic band clasping his temples. A wave of weakness overwhelmed him, and he fell back, down into the nightmare of death and ruin.

CHAPTER TWELVE

There was no hope. Man was lost. *The Hope of Man* was lost. There was no hope . . .

The phrases ran like a child's nursery rhyme through Jerry's mind as he came back to consciousness. When he awoke for the second time his brain was clear, but memories of the dream-images, the cratered streets of London and the dead-alive faces of Cathy and Frank, stayed with him. He raised a hand to his forehead. The metal circlet that had held his head down was gone. With an effort he put aside the thoughts of death and sat up slowly.

He was on a kind of dais against one wall of a large five-sided room. Directly opposite to this dais a tall, narrow doorway led off to unseen regions. Instruments lined the walls, huge dials marked in curving symbols that conveyed nothing to him. Above and between the dials luminiscent panels glowed with a bluish light. In the centre of the floor, six people stood, regarding him intently. The foremost, a stocky, thick-necked man with long dark hair streaked with grey, pointed a peculiar translucent tube at Jerry.

'Stay there!' he ordered gruffly. 'Tell us who you are and what you are doing here.'

Jerry studied the group for a moment before replying. There were four men and two women, all clad in loose tunics and trousers of various colours. All six had light golden skin, and, save for one blonde woman, their hair was black. Altogether, despite their hostile expressions, they were a considerable improvement upon the other inhabitants of the city. His spirits rose.

'I am Colonel Jerry Cornelius, commander of the spaceship which landed on your world two days ago . . .'

The stocky man made a threatening gesture with the tube. 'We do not understand you. Speak in Arvik!'

'Speak in *what*?' Jerry was at a loss.

'Arvik!' growled the spokesman. 'The speech machine taught you while you slept. Speak in our tongue!'

And Jerry realised with a shock that the sounds the other's lips made were strange, but the words which formed in his own brain were clear and familiar. So *that* was the purpose of the metal circlet. A language teaching device! Then the girl who had greeted him when he first awoke had spoken not in English but in Arvik! With the realisation, knowledge of the alien language seemed to leap to his tongue. He repeated his opening words and continued:

'We came from the planet Earth which circles a sun very close to your own solar system. We hoped to find a world similar to Earth. To meet a race so like ourselves is more than we had dreamed.'

He paused. A young man in a yellow tunic turned to the blue-clad spokesman. They began a whispered conversation. Over their heads Jerry saw the girl Lae-Pinu standing in the doorway. She was barefoot and clad in the brief silvery garment he remembered. Her dark eyes were wide and troubled. As his glance met hers, she started and withdrew from sight. The whispering went on. Anxiety finally overrode Jerry's self-control. 'Where is my wife?' he said sharply. 'Where is Cathy? Is she safe?'

The stocky man looked at him coldly. 'There was no woman. I know nothing of any woman. There was only you.'

CHAPTER THIRTEEN

'Stranger!'

Jerry stirred, groaning. His head throbbed. A chill sickness assailed him. Gritting his teeth he braced one arm against the cell wall and rose, fighting down his nausea. Light filtered through the steel-barred window set in the locked door, casting faint shadows upon the stones. Beyond the bars a girl's blonde head was visible, her eyes only just above the level of the window's lower edge. He lurched toward the door.

'Lae-Pinu!' he croaked. 'What's happening?'

'Please!' she whispered. 'Do not make a noise!' She stepped back, glanced swiftly to left and right, came close to the bars again. 'Quickly – take these.'

Two rectangular objects wrapped in some kind of metal foil were thrust through the window. He took them, turned them over in his hands.

'What are they?'

'Food!' Lae-Pinu said. Again she surveyed the corridor. 'They are coming for you soon – my father and the others. He does not believe your story. They will put you before the Judgement Wall to discover the truth.

'I told them the truth!' Jerry gripped the bars in frustration. 'Tell me, has there been any news of my wife?'

'No. I heard my father say that there was no woman among

the Sev-Alab – the creatures of the lower city – when we used the hypnosis machine upon them.'

'But he couldn't be sure,' said Jerry desperately. 'With such a struggle going on and the hypnotic lights flickering, he could have overlooked her! The Sev-Alab may have carried her off when they recovered!'

Lae-Pinu looked to left and right again. 'I do not know –'

He put one hand over hers where she held the grill.

'Lae-Pinu, please, you've got to help . . .'

She started back. 'I must go! If my father finds me here he will punish me! Do not tell him of the food!'

Tears sprang into her dark eyes. Hurriedly, Jerry released her hand.

'I'm sorry,' he said. 'Of course I won't tell your father of this. I should be thanking you for what you've done already, instead of asking more.'

Lae-Pinu looked at him wordlessly for a moment and then she was gone.

Jerry strained his ears for the sound of other footsteps, but heard nothing. He sat against the wall and began to peel off the metal foil. The mere knowledge that food was available filled him with a ravening hunger. He could not remember how long it was since his last meal. It seemed incredible that only weeks ago he had walked across the Gandhi Space Launching Site in company with Cathy and Frank, full of dreams and hopes. The fate of Earth rested on their shoulders, or so the television commentators had declared. Jerry grinned without humour. And here he was, the world's saviour, locked in a cell on a nameless planet. He recalled the scene in the room of the language machine, how he had lost control and attempted to push his way through the group to begin his search for Cathy. The leader had pressed a stud on the translucent tube that he held and Jerry's nerves had burned with a fire so agonising that he sweated at the memory. Then a numbness had enveloped his mind, and he had known no more until the sound of Lae-Pinu's voice awakened him.

The packages held two slabs of a dense, rough-surfaced

substance that smelled faintly of coffee. Nibbling cautiously, he found the flavour quite palatable. The food might be drugged or poisoned, he realised – after all he knew nothing of this race's motives or customs – but he had to trust someone, and the girl seemed sincere. Why was she helping him? Again, without real knowledge of their alien ways, speculation was pointless. Maybe she saw him as an exotic novelty!

Voices echoed in the corridor. Hastily he crammed the last fragments of food into his mouth, crumpled the foil and wedged it into a crevice in the floor. With a last-minute inspiration, he lay down again, huddled in a corner. Sandalled feet slapped upon the stones outside. The lock whirred and a widening wedge of light fell across him. Through half-shut eyes he saw three men in the doorway. A voice said: 'Does he sleep or did the neurogun kill him?'

'Stay back!' came the leader's familiar growl. 'It could be a trick. A touch of the gun will tell us.'

Before Jerry could move a white-hot pain flared in his chest. Mild as it was in comparison to the earlier dose, it still shattered his pretence of unconsciousness. Scrambling to his feet, he stood half-crouched, glaring at his captors. 'What do you want now, you swine?' he shouted, hoarse with thirst and rage. Behind his anger, he coolly noted that the trio retreated a pace at the sight of him.

'Come out!' snapped the leader, flourishing the neurogun. 'It is time for you to stand before the Judgement Wall. The truth of your story will be weighed there before the court of the Sev-Kalan, the people of the upper city. Come!'

Jerry came. They walked in triangular formation, Jerry in the centre, the blue-clad man at the apex behind him, gun in hand. Watery sunlight slanted across the long corridor at intervals, between squat stone pillars. Monstrous carvings covered the walls, leering through the shadows, with an occasional doorway or side-passage to relieve their oppressive weight.

Unconsciously Jerry straightened as they passed into a high open space where the corridor intersected a wide gallery.

They climbed an endless flight of broad steps, came to a crossroads where massive metal doors blocked off all exits save one towering archway. Jerry's heart leaped. The carrier! It stood at the base of a great carved column, the jagged mounting of the broken spotlight glinting in the sunlight. A thrill of hope ran through him. If only he could reach the driving cab –

His footsteps must have faltered. Behind him a voice grated: 'Keep moving!' He gritted his teeth and walked on. Through the archway, and into a room so vast that the several hundred people it held seemed lost and forlorn. Glowing panels lit the lower walls leaving the ceiling shrouded in darkness. As Jerry entered, his eyes were caught and held by an expanse of brass and crystal and rippling colour too great for the mind to grasp. It dominated one end of the cavernous hall, filling the space between with incomprehensible flashing signals. He did not need to be told that this was the Judgement Wall. It was also very obviously a gigantic computer.

A wide aisle led between rows of ornate benches to a tiered platform directly below the Wall. As Jerry strode along, he was acutely aware of hundreds of eyes fastened upon him, of a rising tide of muttering and whispered speculation. The audi-

ence was composed of men and women of all ages and he noticed a few children in the front rows. Tunics were the common dress for young and old. The ever-moving multi-hued beams gave an unreal quality to the scene, masking the contours of the room. He squinted into the rainbow haze, searching for stairways, avenues, exits.

Now the titanic complexity of the Wall was so near that Jerry could no longer discern the outer edges. A sentient mountain, veined with tubes of pulsing light, studded with a myriad trembling instruments cased in brass, it hung above him. For all his familiarity with the giant mechanisms of twenty-first century Earth, he could not repress an irrational fear that the Wall would topple, crushing him beneath its immeasurable weight.

On the highest tier of the platform stood two smooth, black, waist-high blocks. At a command from his gaoler, Jerry walked over to them and turned to face the crowd.

With the watching face of the computer Judge out of sight, he found himself oddly calm. He noticed that the tops of the blocks were worn into shallow depressions, as if by constant rubbing.

The stocky man, standing some distance away with the neurogun still trained upon Jerry, began to address the crowd.

'I speak in the name of the Great Judge. I, Lae-Varka, servant of the Wall, bring the outlander prisoner before the all-seeing eye of the Great Judge, that the truth of his words may be weighed.'

There was a cry of assent from the crowd below. Lae-Varka glanced at the desk console at the further side of the platform and frowned.

'Where is the Keeper of the Records?'

Slowly, reluctantly, Lae-Pinu emerged from the audience and climbed the steps. 'I am here, my father.' She wore now a dark red tunic. Her face was deathly pale, her lips compressed.

Lae-Varka turned to Jerry.

'Prisoner, you may tell your tale. The Keeper of the

79

Records will translate your words into the sacred language of the Great Judge. When all is told, the Voice of the Wall will declare your fate. Stand now between the blocks and place your hands upon them.'

Under the threat of the neurogun Jerry moved to obey. There was a sudden feminine cry.

'Do not touch them! The Wall sends death to those who touch the blocks!'

Heedless of the weapon, Jerry spun about. Lae-Pinu was standing by the console, her face contorted with terror. Her father swung the neurogun, yelling; 'You have broken the Law of the Wall! You are not fit to live!'

He pointed the gun at Lae-Pinu's head.

CHAPTER FOURTEEN

On earth, she would have died. Even as Jerry hurled himself at Lae-Varka, he saw the man's fingers tighten upon the butt of the weapon aimed at the girl's head. It was all very clear and very far away, out of reach. And then his flying body hit Lae-Varka and the smaller man went sprawling.

Gravity was the answer, Jerry thought, while he scrambled to retrieve the neurogun. Two-fifths of one gee, the difference between the pull of this world and Earth, the difference between life and death. A foot came swinging at his head. He dropped flat, caught the foot, twisted it and rolled. The owner crashed to the platform with a startled whoop. Two down and one to go. Lae-Varka, however, was not ready to be counted out. He came up, wild-eyed and breathing hard, as Jerry rose. The sight of the neurogun in the other's hand did not seem to register upon his mind. He rushed in, fingers hooked like claws. The Earthman took one pace forward, pivoted to the right. There was a meaty thud. Lae-Varka fell as if hit by a hammer. Jerry's left fist felt numb. He backed towards Lae-Pinu, bringing the gun to bear upon the audience.

'The next one to move will get this!'

The Sev-Kalan crowded to the base of the platform, surging to and fro as if checked by an invisible wall. He could almost feel their hatred beating up to him in waves. He looked sideways at the girl, at her taut, bloodless face, and realised with a sick horror that the hatred was directed as much at her as at himself. With deliberate curtness, he snapped: 'You know this place – show me a way out! Hurry, girl!'

Lae-Pinu stared back at him. Her throat muscles worked convulsively but no sounds passed her lips. A small bright missile flashed out from the forest of waving arms below and rebounded from the console, missing her by inches. It was a thin-bladed knife. Jerry swallowed his pity, reached out and grabbed Lae-Pinu's tunic shaking her small body like a doll.

'They're going to kill you! Run, girl! Run, damn you! I can't stop them!'

Colour flooded back into her face.

'To the left,' she said. 'The stairway over there leads to an upper gallery –'

He was moving before she could finish the sentence. As they sprinted for the stairway, a roar of fury broke from the crowd. In a multi-coloured wave the Sev-Kalan swept across the platform. Four men appeared at the foot of the steps as if from nowhere. Steel blades glinted. Coldly, Jerry squeezed the neurogun. The crowd, following after, parted and flowed around four stunned, twitching figures. Jerry pounded up the stairway, half-carrying the girl.

From that point onwards, Lae-Pinu took charge. A breathless succession of corridors, ramps and dusty rooms made Jerry's head reel. The howling of the crowd faded, muffled by the intervening stonework. Finally, in a room grimier than any they had previously crossed, Lae-Pinu halted.

'Up there,' she panted, pointing. He looked up. Several feet above his head was a lightless opening roughly two metres high and a metre wide. It looked remarkably like an open grave. Jerry shrugged.

'Right,' he said. 'Up you go, then!'

She placed one foot in his linked hands. He heaved upwards, grunting. She soared with incredible ease, grasped the sill of the opening, and swung herself into it in a flurry of bare golden legs. Jerry backed off, took a short run, and leaped. A moment later, temporarily winded, he was lying beside her in thick, musty darkness. Presently, she tugged gently at his sleeve.

'We can go on, now.'

Jerry sat up. 'No, Lae-Pinu, wait. I must think. I must find my wife. God knows what may have happened to her. If your people haven't got her, then I must search the lower city.'

Her voice sank to a whisper. 'The Sev-Alab do not take people away. When they find someone alone, they kill him and leave the . . . the remains for us to discover. We have placed hypnosis machines and warning signals in all the ways leading from the lower levels, but each year they grow bolder.

He scrubbed the palms of his hands across his face, feeling the unfamiliar rasp of a thickening beard. He was suddenly weary and cold. Dully, he answered: 'Then either your father was mistaken about Cathy not being with the hypnotised Sev-Alab, or someone else has –' He stopped. *Could* someone else have taken her? The words had stirred a dormant memory.

'Lae-Pinu,' he said with a new urgency. 'When Cathy and I were attacked, I thought I saw something just before the hypnotic lights dazzled me. A very tall, manlike figure, barely visible in the shadows. Just standing, like the robot that led us into the city when we first landed on your world. Would the robots hurt a human being, or carry him off?'

'Where . . . where did it go?' she asked, in a voice like that of a frightened child.

'I only saw it for a second or two.' Jerry tried to speak casually, but her tone had filled him with foreboding. 'It didn't move at all. Do you know anything about it?'

'Oh, Jeh-ree!' To his utter amazement and embarrassment, she threw herself against him, making sobbing, incoherent sounds of distress. He held her, letting the tears flow, waiting for her emotions to work themselves out. A small corner of his mind kept hoping that the noise she was making would not attract their pursuers. Presently she calmed and moved away, sniffling. Jerry took a handkerchief from an inside pocket, pressed it into her dimly-seen hand.

'Use this.'

Dabbing her face dry, she said quietly: 'I'm sorry.'

'For what?' he said. 'After what you've gone through in the past hour, you needed to do that. I could shed a few tears myself!'

Crushing down his wild desire to learn the cause of her fear, he put a hand gently on her shoulder.

'Before you tell me what's wrong, lead us out of here. Things may look better in the daylight.'

Lae-Pinu stood up. 'You are not offended when I call you Jeh-ree?'

Jerry chuckled. 'I've been called worse. You have a pretty good memory for names, young lady!'

'I am the Keeper of the Records,' said Lae-Pinu with pride.

A few paces brought them to a metal grating which blocked the narrow tunnel. Despite corrosion, it swung back with little noise when the girl pushed it. Grey light filtered through the dimness from above as they emerged into a circular, vertical shaft that smelled faintly of dampness. High overhead, Jerry saw a pearly disc of sky. Lae-Pinu indicated a ladder of rusty rungs set in the stonework. 'At the top of the shaft we will be in a part of the upper city that has been abandoned. I know it from ancient writings in the Records.'

Jerry stuck the neurogun in his belt, ready to hand.

'Nevertheless, we'll play it safe,' he told her. 'Stay a few rungs below me and keep your head down until I give the all-clear.'

The climb was accomplished without incident. Side by side, Jerry and Lae-Pinu stood upon a wide, windswept roof, drawing deep breaths of cool, moist air. Clouds raced low above the ragged towers that hemmed in their refuge. The sun, just past the zenith, gleamed intermittently through deep blue rifts. No living thing save themselves moved in all that bizarre landscape of stone, but Jerry did not linger. Only when they had found a turret room commanding a view of every possible line of approach did he relax. Lae-Pinu sat beside him in the baroque, crumbling interior, suddenly quiet. For a moment he studied her grave, dust-streaked face, and then he said: 'All right, Lae-Pinu, go ahead. Tell me the worst.'

The Hope of Man was falling. A sleek sentient cylinder of titanium-steel, she slid through the impalpable currents of interplanetary space, her nuclear engines silent. She was falling from apogee to perigee, from the outermost point of her elliptical orbit to the innermost, in a stupendous, suicidal swoop. Frank Marek savoured her fall. He was alive and well and alert. He was exalted and exultant. He was doomed. Weightless, he floated in the disorder of the control-room, staring through an unshielded vision port at the blue-white giant planet falling swiftly astern. He yelled into the dark cavern of the ship: 'Who is your master? Who made you?'

And the ship answered in stunning, echoing amplification: 'Marek! Marek! MAREK!'

Marek laughed. He laughed at Space, at the orange-tinted world he had left, at the wide, encircling Universe. Again he yelled to the ship that was now his creature: 'What is the hope of Man?'

And the ship answered: 'Death! Death is the hope of Man! Death, Death, DEATH!'

Marek was content.

'And so your older sister vanished just as mysteriously as did Cathy?'

Jerry spoke in a whisper. He lay in the narrow horizontal duct of a ventilator, Lae-Pinu at his side. Below them stood the carrier. They had left the turret several hours ago after deciding upon a plan of action, and found their way back to the intersection at the entrance to the Judgement Room. En route they had picked up supplies from the Sev-Kalan warehouses with little difficulty. Now they waited for nightfall, when the upper city would sleep.

'She disappeared four years ago,' Lae-Pinu replied. 'My father had no sons, and so he trained his eldest daughter in the lore of the Wall, for we are the traditional Keepers of the Records. Lae-Mura was his favourite. I had to take her place – it is the law – but he treated me as if Lae-Mura's loss was my fault. I hate him,' she said with quiet intensity. 'I hate the Wall and the whole cruel, stupid business. Sometimes I think that our people are as savage and mad as the beasts of the lower city. If it were not for fear of the Alanga, I would have fled outside the walls long ago.'

Jerry watched a party of Sev-Kalan cross the space below. When they were out of sight, he said: 'I know very little of this world of yours, but I cannot see why the presence of these beings, the Alanga, terrifies the Sev-Kalan. You tell me that they can enter and leave the city at will, and that no one knows how they gain access. They take your people as offerings to some mysterious god called the All-Devourer, according to your records. Yet there is only the vaguest description of them there – tall, slender, moving without sound. Why has there never been an attempt to explore the hills where they are said to live?'

Lae-Pinu shrugged, helplessly. 'We believe that the Alanga would wish us to do this. Then they would fall upon us in the wilderness and destroy us all. Sometimes I feel that would be better than our present existence.'

He noted that her tone was now controlled and rational as she spoke of the beings, in contrast to the near-hysterical account she had given in the turret room when she had finally nerved herself to speak at all. Perhaps he was right, after all, in agreeing to her request to go with him when he made his bid to leave the city. Grimly, he said: 'It's a chance I must take. If Cathy has been taken by the Alanga – and it seems almost certain that she has – I'll scour those hills from end to end, and God help whoever gets in my way!'

When complete silence reigned in the halls and passageways, Jerry uncoiled the rope they had brought, secured one end to a grating and cautiously lowered the other until it brushed the floor. Then, swiftly and stealthily, he descended, followed by the girl. They padded across the wide, cold expanse of paving to the carrier, climbed into the cab. Everything seemed to be in order. Jerry set the engine purring almost inaudibly. No trouble there. He was about to ease the carrier forward when a triumphant shout rang out from the great entrance of the Judgement Hall. With a thunderous, reverberating boom, massive metal doors dropped into place all around, sealing off every avenue.

Lae-Pinu shrieked: 'Jeh-ree! My father has trapped us!'

Sev-Kalan poured from the Hall. At their head was Lae-Varka. In his right hand was the twin of Jerry's neurogun.

'Get down, Lae-Pinu!' Jerry yelled over the clamour of the oncoming mob. 'This is going to be rough!'

As she dropped to the floor of the cab, he gunned the carrier forward, simultaneously triggering the distress siren to full voice. The effect at such close range was shattering. Lae-Varka made a wild, ludicrous attempt to aim the neurogun and cover his ears at the same time. Behind him the other men slowed, bewildered. Lae-Pinu, peering over the rim of the dashboard, cried: 'Where can we go? They have closed all of the doors!'

'That's what your father thinks!' Jerry wrenched the carrier around in a tyre-twisting arc, aligned the nose on the long stairway directly opposite the Judgement Hall. 'Hang on!'

And amid a bedlam of cursing and howling, he drove through the one exit the Sev-Kalan had never thought to close. Lae-Pinu cast one horrified look at the steep stone stops falling endlessly away beneath her, and buried her face in the cushioned seat. The carrier lurched over the brink. Never had Jerry been so acutely aware of sheer speed. The grey walls blurred, flowing by like an enclosing torrent. The six tyres, with their flexible, almost organic structure, absorbed the worst of the repeated shocks, but the jarring and the oscillation of the headlights were unpleasantly similar to the rhythms of the hypnotic machines. It was vertigo quite as much as logic that made him swing the vehicle from side to side of the slope to minimise the sickening pitching motion, converting their descent into a wide snaking series of S-bends. When they bounced off the final step and rolled to a halt in the high gallery he remembered, Jerry had some difficulty in uncurling his fingers from about the steering wheel. He grinned at the dishevelled Lae-Pinu as she opened her eyes and sat up.

'I should have warned you that I used to be a street-car driver in San Francisco!'

'Sehan Francisco . . . what is that?' She was still slightly breathless.

Jerry began to cruise the carrier slowly along the gallery, searching for a continuation of the route down to ground level. 'Sorry! San Francisco is the name of a town on my native planet. Parts of it are built on very steep hills. I went there once with my father when I was a kid.'

'There is more than one town on your world? Why is that?' Lae-Pinu's curiosity overrode her fears. 'Are they like Beya-Sev?'

He was silent for a moment, listening for sounds of pursuit. The engine purred softly and the wheels made a barely audible swish. Otherwise, silence. His mind examined the implications of her questions.

'There are many towns on my world. Surely there are more

than one on yours? Doesn't Beya-Sev have any sort of contact with other communities?'

She looked at him blankly. 'Why would there be other towns? Who would live in them?'

'Who would . . . ?' Jerry did not complete the repetition of her query. He tried to quell an uneasy suspicion about the mental processes of the Sev-Kalan. An old saying ran through his mind: *Everybody's crazy except thee and me – and I have my doubts about thee!*

Aloud, he said: 'On Earth – my world – there are several thousand million people. They live in communities of various sizes, from tiny villages with only a few dozen inhabitants up to great cities holding twenty or thirty millions. Very few cities have a sharply defined boundary like that of Beya-Sev. They sprawl over vast areas and are constantly growing.'

Her eyes were huge with wonder. 'But . . . but . . .' She seemed unable to formulate the question, whatever it was. Half to herself, she murmured: 'All those faces!'

'I know,' said Jerry. 'I feel that way myself.'

CHAPTER FIFTEEN

They were outside the city. It had been easy, after all, so easy that he could still scarcely believe it. The gallery had given them access to a descending ramp and a flat roof. Unwilling to face the dangers of the lower levels during darkness, he had driven across the roof in the hope of seeing some part of the city wall when daylight permitted. To his delight, the roof terminated at the inner surface of the wall, only a foot or so below the parapet. After that it had been a straightforward, if laborious, matter of unshipping the powered winch, anchoring it to a convenient drainage outlet, and allowing the carrier to roll, snail-like, down the slightly sloping outer face of the wall on the end of taut, tough cables. Lae-Pinu's part in the operation had chiefly consisted of standing watch, after a brief lecture on the use of the laser rifle, to see that no person or thing caught them unawares. Nothing did, but the night sounds and smells that rose from the hidden streets of Beya-Sev were not pleasant.

The dawn wind was cold. Jerry, shivering, turned up the heating of his suit. He rummaged in the lockers of the carrier for spare clothing for the girl. She was already hugging herself against the chill, and her legs, little protected by the short red tunic, were covered with gooseflesh. With strands of blonde hair trailing across her face, she had the pathetic look of a lost child. *Which is exactly what she is*, Jerry thought. He pushed the unwelcome thought away. Out here she was safe, at least, from her own people.

'Try this,' he said, holding out Cathy's spare suit. Clumsily she struggled into the unfamiliar garments. Jerry heroically refrained from grinning at the result. Lae-Pinu looked with dismay at the flopping sleeves, the trouser-cuffs trailing over her toes. Tugging at the sagging blouse, she said: 'Thank you. It is very warm.' She carefully folded her tunic and tucked it into the locker. Climbing into the open cab as Jerry slid in behind the steering-wheel, she asked: 'Is your wife very beautiful, Jeh-ree?'

'Very beautiful.' He looked away from her, surveying the dark horizon. In a deliberately lighter tone, he added: 'And very tall, too!'

Lae-Pinu smiled faintly. Then, staring fixedly ahead at the mist-streaked land slowly emerging from night, she whispered: 'I hope the Alanga have not harmed her.'

God help them if they have, Jerry thought savagely. His fingers ran expertly over the control panel. The carrier moved off, drawing broad, glistening tracks across the wet, blue moss. An edge of sun lifted suddenly above the hills, laying orange light on the mist. The windscreen darkened, automatically reducing the glare to a tolerable level, and he flicked off the headlights. At an exclamation from the girl, he looked back. Beya-Sev shone. High overhead the strange, convoluted towers flung back the sun's rays, so blindingly bright that their outlines were already blurred by a shimmer of gold. He had an almost overwhelming impulse to turn back, to ransack the whole fantastic, evil structure for some sign of Cathy. He was deserting her, driving off on a wild hunt on the flimsiest of evidence . . .

'Tell me what you know about the Alanga's homeland,' he said abruptly.

Lae-Pinu drew her gaze from the shining city with reluctance. 'The towers are so beautiful,' she breathed. 'I have never seen them in this way before. If only my people could be here, outside the walls.'

'They could be,' Jerry told her. 'It's my guess that they have shut themselves away in Beya-Sev for so long that they're as much afraid of open spaces as they are of the Alanga.'

'You have not lived in Beya-Sev,'. Lae-Pinu answered with a note of reproof in her voice. 'You have not had to lock doors and set guards every night upon the passageways. After my sister, Lae-Mura, was taken, my mother would not let me out of her sight for weeks.'

'There are many cities like that upon Earth.' He watched the colour of the hills deepen moment by moment, their slopes acquire solidity and perspective. 'There'll be many more if the population keeps on increasing. Now, what can your records tell me about the Alanga?'

'They have secret ways into the city which no-one has ever discovered. My father searched tunnels and passages so old that even the Elders of our council could not recall them having been used, and I studied ancient maps, but we found nothing. There are parts of Beya-Sev which the maps do not show.'

'How do you know that the Alanga live in those hills?' Jerry steered left, skirting a small lake where mist lingered. Something round and green skimmed across the water, sank again with a muffled 'plop'. Feathery black creatures rose from the further shore and flew into the orange haze with curious, barking calls. Lae-Pinu watched them go, and said:

'They have been seen from the upper city. We have a telescope with which our Elders study the lands around Beya-Sev. I remember when I was young seeing a party of Alanga crossing the valley below the hills. It was early in the morning, just like now.'

'Where, exactly?' Jerry asked sharply.

She pointed to the right. 'There – that hill higher than the rest, with streaks of red on its sides. I could not see very much of them, of course, because the telescope is old and doesn't work well.'

Jerry stared at her. 'You're sure they were Alanga? It couldn't perhaps have been a herd of animals, or shadows thrown by moving clouds?'

His voice must have had more of an edge than he had

realised. Her face became sullen. She said, through barely-opened lips: 'Of course they were Alanga! I'm not a liar!' She moved to the other end of the seat and turned her back. Jerry choked down a strong urge to shake her. He contented himself, instead, with saying something brief, in English, to the passing scenery. They rolled on for ten miles more in funereal silence.

The signal came as the carrier was fording the broad, shallow stream that meandered around the stony feet of the hills. On the cab console a blue light began to blink in accompaniment to a series of high-pitched buzzes. Lae-Pinu was jolted from her moody pose as Jerry accelerated, sending the vehicle lunging up the bank, stones scattering from beneath the spinning wheels.

'What is it?' she exclaimed in alarm. 'What has happened?'

'It's her!' Jerry cried. 'It's Cathy! Oh, God, I hope she's all right!'

Lae-Pinu stood up, clutching at the windscreen, and was almost hurled overboard as the carrier swerved. 'Where?' she asked eagerly. 'Where is she?'

He gestured at the console. 'That's her signal. She was carrying a miniature transmitter set to broadcast a distress signal. It can be operated by the wearer, or started automatically by being removed from the wearer's body – she wore it as a pendant. It must be very near – the signal is getting stronger.'

Minutes later he leaped from the cab, ordering Lae-Pinu to remain in the parked carrier to watch the nearby slopes. His face was pale and set as he strode to the edge of the water. The soft mud there had been trampled and churned. Tiny pools had formed in the hollows. The marks were unlike any that he knew, but they were unmistakably those of animals. With cold fingers he groped in the mud and the clumped vegetation, hardly aware that the girl had joined him in his search. It did not take long to find it. Jerry straightened, holding the tiny, exquisitely constructed device and its attached necklace in the palm of his hand. There was mud on it, and something more. Lae-Pinu, coming close, touched the casing with a tentative finger. She looked up at Jerry's drawn, brooding features and said in a small, lost voice: 'The mud . . . it has blood in it!'

CHAPTER SIXTEEN

Marek whimpered. He floated through the curving spaces of *The Hope of Man*, weightless, in free fall. His body was curled in sleep, arms clasping knees, head tucked down upon his chest. A nimbus of dark hair waved about his face. Small things pursued him, borne on the eddying air-currents circulating through the ship. A flask trailed shining globes of liquor which collided constantly, breaking into ever-smaller droplets, creating a universe of mirrors. An endless succession of Mareks, tiny and distorted, revolved with their slow, spinning dance.

The ship murmured. Messages flashed along the intricate network of her electronic nerves. On the control console, screens glowed. Marek stirred, reaching out, groping at the air. His legs moved fitfully. He mumbled.

It was summer, and the broad avenues shimmered with sunlight. Dust eddied about the carefully-spaced trees, rustled on the grey armour of the riot cars parked in their shadow. White-helmeted police slacked in the gun turrets, bored and sweating. Marek ran past them, shouting, his lips cracked and dry. They did not stir. His words died on the hot, still air. The avenue stretched before him interminably, a quivering mirage of glass and concrete, ponderous parallel rows of monuments to a dead political creed that he scarcely remembered. As the rocks swallow and compress green forests and transmute their substance into strange forms, so the pressures of the twenty-first century had seized and warped the social institutions of the twentieth, piling stress upon stress faster than their sagging structures could adjust. But it would all end soon. The world would be clean and clear. Why couldn't he make them hear? Why was his throat so constricted?

The ship was troubled. A programme had been fed into her circuits, locked into her immensely complex computer-brain. In a little while, the huge and beautiful automation that was *The Hope of Man* would enter Phase One of the Warp, the first step into that strange sub-universe of hyper-space beyond the laws of orthodox cosmology. Of all the precautions taken by the gifted scientists who had designed her, working on the sketchiest of information about a region which could not be probed in advance, the most sternly enforced had been that regarding the proximity of matter. No one really knew what might happen if the forces of the Warp were released within the area of distorted space surrounding a sun, but theoretical predictions were apocalyptic enough to deter the rashest of experimenters. Stripped of its esoteric mathematics, the warning had been impressed upon the mind of *The Hope of Man* – stellar mass and the Warp do not mix! And yet her master, Marek, had set her upon the path of destruction, initiating the sequence of spatial re-orientations that would culminate in the shift into hyperspace, while her present orbit led her with increasing speed toward the small planet that burned, remote and bright, in her vision screens. The ship was troubled, but meanwhile there were dangers that she could deal with. Her defences went into action.

He had used his native tongue only rarely during the twenty years that had elapsed since he emigrated to the Californian Republic, and it was strange now to hear it all about him. The avenue was thronged with men, women and children, clad in the gay, casual clothes that were the universal form of summer dress. Flowers on a coffin lid, Marek thought, as he pushed his way through the crowd. He had come home, back to the continent of his youth, bearing a message. The message was liberation, liberation beyond the feeble dreams of the revol-

*utionaries who roved Asia and the American States. The final
liberation. The bombs were coming, the multi-headed missiles,
the nuclear rain that would wash the earth, sterilise it, cleanse it
of the squirming, pullulating mass that was humanity. He came
to a vast open square surrounding the pedestal of a statue built
on a scale of paranoiac grandeur. Standing amid the unheeding
strollers, he cried his news, arms outflung to the sky. And it was
true. The sky vanished, was wiped away by a fire intolerably
bright that burned through his closed eyelids as the bombs
exploded and exploded and exploded . . . . . .*

Marek awoke screaming. The screens above him flickered
with brilliant, intermittent flashes as the atomic shield of the
ship intercepted and vaporised fragments of rock and metal,
the debris of the planet-forming processes, streaming eter-
nally around the distant orange sun. There was nothing there
to deflect him from his course. He shook his head as if to clear
his vision, and looked across the Control Room at the chronometer. Phase One was near.

CHAPTER SEVENTEEN

'Jeh-ree?'

Jerry Cornelius looked away from the tiny transmitter resting in his palm. Lae-Pinu was watching him with an expression of concern. He realised that she had spoken to him more than once.

'I'm sorry,' he said. 'You were right, Lae-Pinu. The Alanga, whatever they are, do exist.' He turned the device over, as if some fresh information might be gained by doing so. 'We've got to assume that Cathy was wearing this up to the time it fell beside the stream. Let's examine the place for other signs.'

They found the second group of prints almost immediately. Smaller, and sunk more deeply into the mud than were the others, they were plainly the tracks of a quadruped. At one point they had been obliterated by a broad furrow. Unskilled as he was in the art of reading signs, Jerry still felt fairly confident in assuming a solitary animal dragged down by a hunting pack. What sort of hunters, he wondered, and what was their prey? The unbidden thought came to him: had the object of the struggle been Cathy?

'There do not seem to be any marks made by people,' Lae-Pinu said, hopefully. She moved her feet up and down as she spoke, apparently enjoying the feel of the mud between her toes.

'That's true,' Jerry agreed, smiling. 'Let's take that as an indication we're on the right trail.' He felt illogically cheered by her words. 'Hop back in the carrier, girl, and we'll take a look at the hill where you saw the Alanga. Wipe your feet first!'

She laughed, the first real expression of amusement that he had seen from her since first they met. She was, Jerry decided, a very pretty girl.

'It sucks, doesn't it?' She said, scrubbing at her feet with a handful of blue moss.

Jerry climbed into the driving seat. 'The mud? Yes, I suppose it does. My paddling days are long gone! Is this the first time you've ever stood on natural ground?'

Lae-Pinu nodded. 'There are a few small gardens in the upper city, but they are mostly dried up and withered. My mother told me that *her* mother had seen living flowers once in a garden, but that was long ago.'

He backed the carrier away from the stream and turned it toward the hill with the red-streaked flanks that she had indicated. The slope was fairly gradual at first and they made good speed, climbing diagonally across the face of the range. It was close to high noon of this world's eighteen-hour day, but the air was cooled to a pleasant degree by a breeze off the hills. Vegetation thickened as they climbed, tough, slender trunks quite unlike the forests of the plateau, tangled and matted with wiry stems that bore black fruit. When he was

forced to bulldoze his way through patches too extensive to make detouring practical, Jerry felt a quite unreasonable twinge of guilt as stems snapped and fell. Conditioned by his early training in the science of nutrition to regard plant life as something to be nurtured and protected, constantly outraged by the thoughtless burning and mutilation inflicted upon the Earth's oldest living things, the trees, he found it difficult to make a virtue of present necessity. To Lae-Pinu, on the other hand, the ride was clearly the greatest thing that had ever happened.

A thousand feet above the plain, they halted on an open, rocky ledge that commanded a view both upslope and down. Jerry swung out of the cab and stretched, breathing deeply. Walking to the edge of the rocks, he stared out across the flat immensity of the plateau to where the city lay like a discarded piece of jewellery, gleaming through the faint orange haze. The girl joined him, though she refrained from approaching the very brink of the drop. Jerry covertly studied her reaction to the panorama below.

'The city is so *small*,' she said quietly.

'Like your world or mine, seen from space,' Jerry answered. 'But all the people, and their problems, remain as big as ever.' Struck by a sudden thought, he said: 'What is the name of your world? You never told me.'

'Why, Beya, I think . . . I'm not really sure. Do all worlds have names?'

Once again, he was thrown mentally off-balance by her naivety. He explained the origins of various planetary names to her, meanwhile speculating inwardly upon this new information. If Beya was a world, was Beya-Sev a 'world-city'? And if so . . . He decided it was time to eat.

Lae-Pinu was fascinated by the many-coloured concentrates and liquids which had originally been carried in the deep-freeze compartments of *The Hope of Man*, and at first did not realise that they were edible. Jerry, picking up a chunk of the coffee-scented substance taken from the city storerooms, asked incredulously: 'Is this the only form of food available in Beya-Sev?'

Licking a drop of pink ice-cream off her upper lip, she said: 'The Great Judge has told us that it is all we need. It has always been there and always will be. Without it we would be like the Sev-Alab, the beasts of the lower city. By processes known only to the Great Judge, the elements of the food are drawn from water and air and rock.'

103

My God, thought Jerry, it's like one of those old commercials from the days when some countries had so much food that people had to be seduced into eating it. He didn't ask what the diet of the Sev-Alab consisted of. He didn't really want to know. But he made a resolve to analyse the food as soon as circumstances permitted. After sampling it while a prisoner of the Sev-Kalan, he could vouch for its nutritional value. And the available food sources of Earth were all too few. Fine, said a small sardonic voice within him, all you have to do now is get it back there.

When evening came, the carrier was forging steadily upward on the steepening sides of the supposed Alanga hill. Spiny ridges, stained rust-red by minerals leached from upper slopes, jutted through the gnarled and gloomy thickets. Jerry had just begun to debate the wisdom of making camp for the night when a crackling rush of unseen bodies through the darkness ahead brought his heart into his mouth. He flicked on the headlights. Frozen almost in mid-stride, a group of weird beings looked blindly back at him with huge, dazzled yellow eyes. The tableau lasted no more than seconds. On legs – or were they legs and forearms? – that must in the larger specimens have been all of six feet long, they resumed their headlong flight into the scrub. Mournful, hooting cries drifted back to the two travellers. When Jerry's pulse had slowed to something like its normal rate, he said: 'If those were your friends the Alanga, our chief difficulty will be catching them!'

'Oh no, they cannot be the Alanga. I have never heard of creatures like that before.' Her voice was utterly serious.

With equal seriousness, he answered: 'It's what may be chasing them that worries me. Be ready to use this.'

He passed the neurogun to her. She was in the act of reaching for it when the deep blue arch of sky above seemed to burst apart. Light cascaded upon the hills, the plateau, the whole visible world. Colour vanished. The universe was molten silver and blackest ink. And silence. No thunder followed, no shock wave. Space, thought Jerry incoherently, even as he crouched numbly in the carrier's cab, explosion in space. Must have been outside the atmosphere or there would be blast. He heard Lae-Pinu shouting and saw, through watering eyes, some kind of struggle raging around the vehicle. His body responded to danger instinctively, but his mind had room for only one terrible, over-whelming realisation – *The Hope of Man* was gone!

CHAPTER EIGHTEEN

The Hope of Man was gone! Jerry shook his head as if recovering from a blow. There was no time for despair. As the light of the great explosion faded from the sky, and his eyes began to function normally again, he saw a confusion of leaping, plunging bodies all around the carrier. Beasts and riders! The latter were undoubtedly human, their tall shapes wrapped in robes and leather. Several gripped short spears, while other weapons swung at their sides, slings, stone-tipped maces, bows. Their mounts were bizarre, high-backed and slim-legged with pendulous blue crests surmounting their narrow heads, a heavy fleece covering them almost to the feet. No rider had yet been unseated, but they were plainly having immense difficulty in controlling their fear-maddened beasts.

'The Alanga! The Alanga!' Lae-Pinu was clutching his arm, her mouth only inches away from his ear.

'You could be right!' Jerry shouted over the hubbub. He put the carrier into motion, heading uphill. 'Whoever they are, I prefer to talk to them from a distance. Let's be off while they're busy.'

For good measure, he sounded the distress siren and turned on every available light. As the carrier roared toward a gap in the scrub, the nearest mounts sheered away in panic. They had a brief glimpse of a rider's hawk-like face as he swayed far out, clinging to his beast's thick wool and waving a spear. Jerry swung around him, expecting at any moment to feel a heavy point tearing into his flesh. Low branches raked across the windscreen. Wood splintered. The wheels rode up over tilted rocks, dropped jarringly to earth again. The tyres took a fresh grip, the superb engine responded, and within seconds they were clear of the disordered ambush. He did not stop until they had a large area of open space around them.

'Jeh-ree . . . Jeh-ree . . .' Lae-Pinu stopped, gulped for air. He could feel a fine trembling in her body as she rested against him. Two shocks so close together, he guessed, had produced an equally strong reaction. He put an arm about her shoulders, held her while the shaking subsided. Meanwhile, his eyes never left the broad stretch of hillside that lay below them, brilliantly lit by the headlamps. Voices and the snorting of animals drifted up the slope, but as yet no sign of pursuit. Despite the warm proximity of the girl, Jerry was suddenly acutely aware of loneliness. What was he doing on this alien hill, with a band of armed riders about to fall upon him? Where was Cathy? The destruction of *The Hope of Man*, being stranded upon this hostile world – all this could be borne if only she was safe, if only he could find her. He felt a fleeting pang of sorrow for Frank Marek. Something very terrible had happened to that courageous and brilliant scientist in the strange, distorted universe of hyperspace. Had that quality of misanthropy apparent in his nature, expressed chiefly in his ironic jokes about mankind's dreams of Utopia, been unchained, set free to dominate his reason? Might it be that Jerry and Cathy had suffered less grievously because of their rapport, the check-and-balance effect of contrasted but complementary personalities? He stared into the night, blinking away the weariness that weighted his eyelids. The fate of Earth was a far-away thing, abstract and unreal. Reality for the moment was Beya and a tall girl with auburn hair.

*   *   *

It was fortunate for Field Marshal Hira that the light which rushed outward from the Centaurian system at one hundred and eighty-six thousand miles per second would not reach his eyes for another four years, if at all. That brief, abnormal burst of energy, so different to the cold unchanging glitter of the distant suns, would have brought to his keen mind the same message that had appalled Colonel Jerry Cornelius. He paced the upper promenade of the Control Centre Building, high above the silicon-concrete desert of the Gandhi Space Launching Site. White moonlight washed the artificial plain and the barren lands beyond. The burning heat of an Indian day had ebbed into the higher air, and a cool night breeze ruffled Hira's silvery hair. He walked with hands clasped behind his back, his brown eyes thoughtfully regarding the scarred beauty of the full moon. As on many other such nights, he fancied that he could discern, at the limit of vision, the cruciform pattern of Lunar One, the greatest concentration of research laboratories in the Solar System. From that point the eye of his imagination leaped, across meaningless millions of miles, to the triple fires of Centauri.

He realised, as never before, how difficult it was to *believe* in the stars. Traverse the planetary orbits, from the searing hell of sunward Mercury to the frozen solitude of Pluto, and the stars remained the same. Aloof, remote – and inaccessible? Not now, Hira told himself, not now. A few months more and the stars will be ours. If we can hold civilization together until then. Along the promenade a door slid open, sighed shut again. A tall, heavily-built man emerged from the shadows, walking with precise, rapid strides. Hira paused.

The big man halted, saluted with a well-judged blend of formality and familiarity. 'Perimeter report, sir.'

'Yes, Major Armstrong?' Hira, sensing trouble, tried to read some meaning into the impassive Occidental face. As usual, he failed.

'Pressure building up on Sector Yellow North, sir. It could be nasty if it continues. Lieutenant Bruckner did a minicopter survey and says he spotted a Church of Relativity cell stirring things up. They're mostly states people in that sector, sir, with a few New Australasians. A bad mixture.'

Field Marshal Hira nodded. 'Any mixture that includes the Church of Relativity is a bad one. Einsteinian Fundamentalists are all we need to have a major action on our hands.' He began to walk toward the nearest doorway. 'You have the record with you? Good. Run it through in here.'

In the softly-lit, deserted room, Major Armstrong took a small plastic container from his pocket, clipped it into one of the visualisers which were standard fixtures throughout the Control Centre. At the touch of a switch, colour and movement flooded into the viewing prism. A Lilliputian three-dimensional version of the launching site flowed swiftly by as the remote-control camera in the tiny helicopter scanned the earth below. Yellow beacons gleamed ahead, spaced out along a tall metal-mesh fence that marked off the spacefield from the brown, dry plain. To right and left, diminished by distance, the lights of Sectors Red and Green glowed. Across the fence, all semblance of order was lost. Tents, inflatable plastic domes, motor-caravans, a hundred varieties of portable housing, darkened the plain for mile upon mile. Rivers of luminous colour ran through the huddled structures, winding along unplanned, crooked courses. Major Armstrong jabbed a thick forefinger at the prism.

'Watch them, sir, when I step up the magnification.' He manipulated the visualiser controls, brought the scene rushing up toward them. Individual faces could be distinguished in the long processions that shuffled by. High above the heads of the crowd, illuminated signs bobbed on the ends of insulated poles. Hira read the gaudy inscriptions silently.

'THERE IS NO UNIVERSE BUT EINSTEIN'S' ... 'HYPERSPACE INVASION WILL DESTROY THE BALANCE OF CREATION' ... 'HOLES IN SPACE WILL SWALLOW OUR EARTH!' ...

'EINSTEIN EQUALS SANITY – HYPERSPACE IS HELL'.

There were other, less coherent slogans, in a score of languages. A vast, formless chanting filled the loudspeaker, mingled with clashing strains from numberless musical instruments. Black, yellow, brown and white faces looked up to the hovering television eye. Anger deepened the wordless sounds that rose from the myriad throats, fists were raised, objects soared and fell back upon the surging mob. Flame stabbed suddenly, searingly bright. The eye swept about in a tight curve and headed back to the towering mass of Control Centre. The prism went dark.

'Those flashes,' Hira said, 'were laser pistols.'

Armstrong straightened. 'There were at least two rifles among them, too. For a movement that apparently didn't exist until a year ago, the Church of Relativity is remarkably well-equipped, sir.'

Hira's brown eyes were hooded and introspective. He walked slowly to the door. Out on the promenade, he said: 'How many people are around the field now?'

'At the last count, two million. The Einsteinians represent perhaps one-fifth of the total. Aerial reports estimate another million or so within a seventy-mile radius, converging upon the Site. Without the electrified fence there wouldn't be an unoccupied square yard of concrete by now.'

'Two million . . .' Field Marshal Hira shook his head. In a voice that Armstrong had to strain to hear, he murmured: 'What do they *want*? What do they think we can do? How do they propose to live out there?'

'They won't live, sir,' Armstrong answered bluntly. 'Some of the first arrivals, the ones who were here when *The Hope of Man* took off, before we had to erect the fence, are starving. They won't accept food or medical aid from anyone. They just wait.' He wheeled, looked squarely at his commanding officer. 'I'm not worried about them, not from a military point of view. It's the later arrivals, the crackpot organizations, the private armies, such as the Church of Relativity, that are the real threat. They've got the death-wish, or whatever the therapists call it nowadays, the will to destroy. God knows what satisfaction they get from it. But we'll stop them, sir, we'll stop them. Thank the Lord we have realists at the top of the United Nations in *this* century!'

Hira did not answer. From the distant perimeter came a rattle of gunfire. Lasers flashed. Three huge helicopters lifted from an unseen pad, rumbled away across the field. Flame blossomed somewhere beyond the fence and a pillar of oily smoke climbed between the watchers and the moon. The major swore. Hira snapped: 'Major Armstrong, there is to be no firing back! Use sleep-gas if the fence is breached and have squads stand by to carry the rioters off the field before they recover. I'll courtmartial any man, whatever his rank, who opens fire without a direct order from me!' He looked at the stars, those distant suns. Whatever *The Hope of Man* returns to, he thought, it won't be to a field reddened with the blood of frightened, deluded men, not so long as I retain command. I think you would call that a realistic attitude, Colonel Cornelius. We're the same kind of realist, you and I. But hurry – for the sake of humanity, hurry!

CHAPTER NINETEEN

'We can talk from here,' Jerry said. He stood in the carrier's cab, one hand resting lightly on the laser rifle. At the edge of the scrub a rider sat his restless mount, his spear laid across the saddle. Between Earthman and Beyan ran a long, black, smoking furrow in the soil. Jerry pointed to it.

'You see what this weapon can do. I come in peace, seeking a lost companion. I have no wish to hurt anyone, but those who would bar my way must take the consequences.'

He spoke in slow, carefully enunciated Sev-Kalan. Lae-Pinu had been astounded to discover that she shared a common language with the barbaric strangers, but to Jerry it meant the confirmation of certain theories he had formed about this world. As he waited for a reply. He kept a keen watch upon the riders bunched behind their spokesman, but they seemed content to wait on the outcome of the exchange.

'Beware, Jeh-ree!' the girl gasped suddenly. Jerry tensed at the same instant, as the Beyan began to raise the spear. Then, leaning forward over the animal's neck, he plunged the point into the ground. Straightening, he spread both arms wide, showing empty hands. In the glare of the headlamps, he was an imposing figure, taller and heavier than the Earthman, with flowing beard and shaven skull. Loose robes emphasized his bulk. Sonorously, his oddly accented words rolled across the intervening space.

'Man of a far land, we too are men of peace. I, Chailemm, speak for all when I say that we make you welcome. But know that there is no place for machines in our community, and the makers of machines. You must put aside these devices of evil, or perish, man and woman alike.' He folded his arms and sat, a dark, monolithic figure of menace, in the saddle. 'That is my word – I, Chailemm, Speaker for the Alanga!'

'Do not believe him, Jeh-ree!' Lae-Pinu said, imploringly. She looked from Jerry to the huge, motionless figure of the Alanga spokesman, her young face mirroring a struggle between trust and superstitious fear. 'He is trying to trick you into surrendering your rifle! Then they will make prisoners of us for their evil god, the All-Devourer!'

Without glancing down, Jerry patted her shoulder. 'Maybe he's lying, maybe not. Either way, Chailemm is a brave man, because he knows I could burn him down with this laser at any moment.' His voice took on a grimmer note. 'I'm inclined to believe him. But I'm not parting with the carrier or the rifle, not for any man or nation on Beya! *The Hope of Man* has gone, but Cathy still has to be found, and until that happens I go armed!'

'Stranger, what is your decision?' The deep tones were edged with impatience, though the man had not moved.

How much does he know, Jerry wondered, how deep is his ignorance of science? Can I bluff him into letting us go without bloodshed? Surely his people can have no conception of the cause of the explosion they've just seen? He spread his arms wide, empty palms showing plainly, in imitation of the Alanga's gesture.

'Speaker Chailemm, men of the Alanga, you have guessed correctly that I come from a far land. What you do not guess is that my land lies on another world, a world similar to your own, called Earth. My name is Jerry Cornelius, and I represent the people of Earth who built the great ship in which myself and my companions voyaged through space. We come in peace, to warn you of a danger which threatens your people, and mine. You have just seen the first omen of that danger in the sky.'

116

Now there was a stirring among the shadowy riders grouped beneath the branches. Several shot quick, seemingly apprehensive looks at the star jewelled darkness overhead. Chailemm did not even turn his head.

'The girl has not come from this world you speak of, this Earth. She is of the Sev-Kalan, the people of the city. How does she come to be in your company, Jericornelius?'

There's nothing wrong with your eyesight, *Chailemm*, thought Jerry. Aloud, he said: 'As our ship circled your world, we saw the city from above. We were seeking for signs of intelligent life, and so we came to Beya-Sev in the hope of finding beings with whom we could exchange information. However, the inhabitants were none too willing to help us. Catherine – my wife – vanished from the city, and if it had not been for the courage of Lae-Pinu who has accompanied me, I would have been a prisoner there, or worse.'

'So you think to find your wife in the hills, Jericornelius? Why should she be here?'

There was an undertone to the question, an extra shade of meaning that the Earthman sensed but could not pin down. Or was fatigue making his mind suspect subtleties where none existed? He sighed. Instead of exchanging fruitless cross-talk while Cathy faced God knew what dangers, how temptingly easy it would be to blast a way through these barbarians and pursue his own path into the night!

A split second later he regretted his indecision. With the faintest of hisses, a noosed rope flashed out of the darkness behind him like a striking snake. A violent tug pulled him off his feet and he thudded into the driving seat, half-winded. Lae-Pinu sprang across him, grabbing the butt of the laser rifle. He caught a glimpse of her pale face, her dark eyes, wide and wild. The laser beam carved the upper air, scattering shadows across the slope. Animals squealed in terror, fighting away from the blinding ray, throwing their riders into confusion. Jerry fought frantically against the pull of the rope, his arms bound tightly against his sides, rage and despair goading his weary muscles. Lae-Pinu steadied the rifle, swept it down. A knotted cluster of branches exploded into flame above

117

Chailemm's head as he struggled to control his mount. He leaped from the saddle, sending the shambri galloping to safety with a powerful smack on the rump. At that instant, a second noose encircled the girl's shoulders and jerked her, threshing and sobbing to join Jerry on the seat. The stealthy Alanga ropemen who had come upon them unseen, now sprang into the cab and began, very efficiently, to tie their arms and wrists. Lae-Pinu fought with feet and teeth and voice until the men, not ungently, trussed her ankles, too.

'I'm sorry, Lae-Pinu,' said Jerry, 'I'm sorry.' It sounded silly and useless even in his own ears, but she smiled while tears of anger still glistened on her cheeks.

'It is not your fault, Jeh-ree. Do not blame yourself.'

Chailemm, mounted again, rode up alongside the carrier. He looked down at them from his great height, his bearded face enigmatic. Turning in the saddle, he shouted to the riders forming up once more on the hillside.

'Galdonn! Sechral! Come, take the man and woman on your shambri. But beware – the beasts may not like the smell of the strangers!'

That detached, observing portion of Jerry's mind that continued to function even at the times of great stress, noted a new word. Shambri had not been part of the Sev-Kalan vocabulary implanted in his brain by the city's language-machine. Another indication that the Alanga and the city-dwellers had diverged from a common cultural beginning? Yet how, in the name of Creation, could a planetary culture consist of one mechanized community and a band of hill-dwelling hunters?

Snorting and stamping, two blue-crested shambri approached the carrier, their riders urging them forward with nudges and soothing words. The nearer Alanga was a smaller version of Chailemm, broad-shouldered and heavy, his youthful features half-hidden by a thick black beard. At his side rode a man several years his junior, slim and upright, his bright blue eyes unashamedly taking in every detail of the two prisoners and their vehicle. As the beasts, with skittish re-luctance, came close to the cab, the younger man somehow contrived to place his mount between that of his companion and the carrier's side. It could have been accidental, but Jerry, noting the fleeting scowl that passed over the other's face, thought otherwise. The ropemen looked doubtfully from one man to the other, obviously wondering which of them to obey, but the interloper, grinning said: 'Leave the heavier burden to my brother Galdonn – his are the broader shoulders!'

Lae-Pinu had ceased to struggle and lay like a dead weight as the hunters lifted her. Sechral reached down and gathered her from their arms with an easy strength that belied his slightness. As her tight-lipped, tear-streaked face under its tousled mop of blonde hair came level with his own, he said lightly: 'The Sev-Kalan are indeed crazy to allow their prettiest daughters to roam the hills at night! Or have they finally decided to quit that middle-heap on the plain and come out into the air?'

She spat at him. Laughing, he placed her, side-saddle, on the shambri's back, holding her with an arm about her waist. Turning away from the carrier, he called to Galdonn: 'Take care, brother – do not tell yours that he has a pretty face! He may spit venom!'

119

Galdonn's reply was another, and even more interesting, example of cultural divergence. Then he dragged Jerry up like a sack and growled: 'Hold to the fleece and do not try to dismount until I say so!'

Chailemm's deep tones rose above the noise of men and animals, and for a moment there was stillness.

'It is time that we were gone. Harn, the White One, will rise before morning and the Drigg will hunt by his light. It is not a propitious time to meet them, for their numbers will be many. Let us go!'

The shambri broke into long, smoothly-swinging strides. Twisting his head about, Jerry had a final sight of the carrier, empty and silent, still blazing its headlamps into the tangled scrub. Presently, low-hanging branches intervened. The riders rounded a jagged wall of rock, and there was nothing more to be seen.

CHAPTER TWENTY

'In the name of the Great Judge, woman, be silent!'

Lae-Varka thumped the table with the flat of his hand, making the dishes rattle. Particles of food sprayed from his lips. The small blonde woman seated at the far side of the room shook her head wearily, as if observing a familiar scene. Her reply, delivered in a low, monotonous whine, had the mechanical quality of a statement made many times before.

'Anger will not change the truth, husband. Our youngest daughter is gone, driven away by your cruelty. Now we have lost both of our children. Without someone to carry on the duties of the Varka, what will become of us? We are nothing . . . nothing!'

The stocky man wiped crumbs from his beard, violently.

Do you think I do not know that – I, the Voice of the Great Judge, whose ancestors have served the Wall since Beya-Sev began? If you had given me sons instead of –'

He broke off at the sound of running feet in the corridor outside. A loud knocking followed. The woman rose and slid aside the bronze-panelled doors, admitting a slim man in yellow tunic and trousers. Agitatedly he bowed and then trotted to Lae-Varka's side.

'Well, Lahl-Maghra, what is it, man? Speak, speak!'

'Speaker,' Lahl-Maghra panted. 'There is something wrong at the Wall! The Great Judge has given strange signals – we do not know what he required of us!'

'Ha!' Lae-Varka barked. 'The Elders may mumble and mutter that there is no place for a Speaker whose wife cannot give him heirs, but who do they run to when in doubt?' The woman began to speak. He waved a dismissing hand at her. 'Be silent, wife! This is a man's business. Come, Lahl-Maghra!'

Once in the corridor, the acolyte's agitation became something closer to panic. At an angle of the passage, he paused and began to babble his story, but Lae-Varka pushed him ahead, saying brusquely: 'Whatever it is, it can wait until we reach the Judgement Hall. I take it that the Elders still have tongues in their doddering heads!'

It required a massive effort of will to keep his facade of confidence intact when finally he strode through the towering doorway of the Judgement Hall and confronted the scene within. Seated on the dais below the vast face of the Great Judge, the six Elders of the Sev-Kalan were submerged in a sea of sombre yellow light, the colour of imminent peril in the code of the Wall. All other signals had disappeared. The few members of the community still awake at this hour were huddled in a small dark group in the front pews. Lae-Varka paced unhurriedly up the central aisle, ignoring their pallid, staring faces. Two women sobbed, somewhere in the gloom. He mounted the steps to the dais.

'What news have you?' He addressed the Elders without formality, noting, not for the first time, that the marks of senility were upon them, despite the fact that there was little difference in years between himself and the youngest of the six. Surely a man's life had been longer when Beya-Sev was newly built?

'You speak discourteously, but we forgive your error, for the occasion is one to disturb the reason of the strongest of men.' The speaker was Borud-Brahn, oldest member of the upper city tribe. The careful phrasing of his rebuke could not disguise the quaver in his voice. Slumped in his chair, he regarded Lae-Varka with faded, watery eyes. 'We can tell you little, other than what you see for yourself, Less than one quarter of an hour ago, the yellow signals began to cover the

Wall. We await your interpretation of the words of the Great Judge.'

Lae-Varka nodded. Seated at the desk console, he fell easily into a routine that he had not practised in several years, ever since his daughter had become Keeper of the Records. The information flowed from the vast storage banks of the Wall, becoming comprehensible as the console transformed the symbols into the language of men. Slowly, Lae-Varka's expression grew grim. Presently he rose and faced the silent assembly.

'What is the word of the Great Judge . . .' Borud-Brahn's query tailed off into inaudibility.

'The message,' said Lae-Varka harshly, 'is that within two nights and two days, Beya-Sev will be destroyed!'

CHAPTER TWENTY-ONE

The black beast paused upon the crest of the ridge, sniffing the air. Light from the huge pale planet on the horizon silvered the stiff ruff of hair that bristled upon its thick neck. As it swung its blunt, fanged snout from side to side, two red feral pin-points glowed under the heavy brows above the flaring nostrils. For a moment it stood, testing the rich odours that flooded from the tangled vegetation on the hillside. Then the muscular body stiffened. A low mewing issued from the barely-open jaws. Where there had been only shadows, there was suddenly a pair, a quartet, a dozen black shapes. They coalesced, became a pack, flowed across the open ground toward the scrub.

'Slowly . . . slowly,' Chailemm murmured, as he rode alongside the trail leader of the Alanga band. 'If the Drigg are hunting tonight, this will be their hour. There is much fresh spoor to draw them.'

The gaunt rider nodded. 'Even so, Chailemm. The shambri are becoming uneasy.' He patted the thick fleece on his mount's arching neck. 'Trust these ears and long nose to give warning.'

'When the Drigg hunt, I trust nothing.' Chailemm turned his shambri about, rode back down the line of plodding animals. Reaching one that was doubly burdened, he said quietly: 'How goes it, stranger?'

Jerry Cornelius glared at him. 'It goes badly. What else do you expect with these on my wrists?' He flourished his bound hands before the Speaker's eyes, and was forced to make a hasty grab at the shambri's fleece to prevent himself from pitching out of the saddle.

Behind him the hunter, Galdonn, cursed. Craning his head around the Earthman's taller form, he growled: 'How long must my beast suffer this fellow's weight? Cannot he be passed to someone else?'

'A reasonable request,' said Chailemm. In a low but carrying voice, he called to a nearby rider. 'Genli! Take the outlander upon your saddle to ease Galdonn's mount. Steady, now . . . take it slowly.'

An amused chuckle sounded from the darkness close at hand. 'Galdonn, my brother, you lack the quality of sympathy for this task. See how mine sleeps!'

And indeed Lae-Pinu did sleep, betrayed by her own weariness, her blonde head lolling on Sechral's shoulder. Galdonn's thick, black eyebrows drew together in a frown, but he said nothing, concentrating upon the awkward business of transferring Jerry from his own shambri to that of Genli. When the exchange was completed, he muttered: 'Harn be thanked!' and promptly edged away. With Genli's hand to steady him, Jerry eased himself gingerly into the saddle. He had never cared for horseback riding, and the

movement of the shambri was markedly more unsettling that that of any terrestrial animal he had ever sat. Scarcely had he gripped the neck-fleece when there came a sudden rustling in the bushes ahead. The shambri made a thin, bleating sound, and abruptly jerked its head up. Jerry slid sideways, fingers knotted in the shaggy pelt, muscles bulging with strain. Somewhere in

126

the night, the trail leader blew two short, urgent notes on a carved horn.

'The Drigg hunt!' Genli's voice sounded, low-pitched and intense, in Jerry's ears. Without further signals, the Alanga drew together, forming a wedge. Spear-points bristled along its edges. Chailemm and the gaunt leader formed the apex, each with bows strung and arrows nocked. Unnoticed save by Sechral, Lae-Pinu awoke and gazed bewilderedly at the warlike scene. A clearing opened before the riders, and as they rode out into the white light of Harn, she seemed fully to recollect the situation. Sechral pressed her close as she instinctively attempted to draw away.

'Sit quietly, little one. There is danger all around us. Be still, and do not distract me from my duties.' He spoke gently, almost casually, but his grip was unbreakable. She twisted her head about to look up at him. There was a half-smile on his dark, beardless face. His blue eyes flicked a brief glance at her, then returned to their scrutiny of the hillside. The bushes rustled again, and she felt a swift stab of fear.

With a crash, the tall stalks immediately before Chailemm collapsed. Giant figures shouldered through, trampling the foliage, brushing broken stems aside. The trail leader flung out his arms, crying: 'Hold! Hold! Mahra! Mahra!'

'What is it?' Jerry asked, striving to see over the heads of the intervening riders. 'What's happening?'

He had his answer almost before Genli could begin to reply. Into the clearing ran a band of familiar beings. Saucer-sized yellow eyes gleamed from simian faces, incredibly long fore-arms swung in unison with the shorter, sturdier hind-legs. The creatures loped across the open ground, uttering gabbling sounds of distress. Clinging to the long hair on the shoulders of several were their young, lightly-furred and unsettlingly humanoid. Jerry knew them now. A band like this had crossed the path of the carrier only hours before. No-one tried to intercept them.

'They are the Mahra, outlander, the people of the forest,' said Genli, no longer whispering. 'Except at birthing time,

127

they are harmless. But be ready, now, for tonight they are the quarry of the Drigg. Brace yourself!'

Something black came out of the forest. The horn brayed, high and hard. Polished stone spearheads lifted, gleaming dully. The Drigg cast a look of crimson-eyed malevolence at the waiting beasts and men, and then ignored them. Lifting its head to the sky, it cried out, a high screaming that ended in a sound like the ripping of heavy cloth. Jerry's stomach contracted. Was this *thing* the source of the tracks where Cathy had crossed the stream? Sweat broke out upon his back and palms.

There was a sudden sound of indrawn breath, a collective movement of the shambri. The Drigg sprang. It seemed fantastically to multiply itself, becoming a twelve-headed fury. The Mahra scattered in panic, hopelessly. Jerry saw one female stumble. She recovered almost instantly, but the cub she carried had lost its grip upon her hair, and rolled over and over across the rocky ground. Under the very feet of Sechral's mount a Drigg pounced, crunched the cub's skull with yellow fangs. Lae-Pinu shouted as the shambri reared, kicking and snorting. A foot caught the killer's blunt dark head. With blood-chilling speed the Drigg twisted aside and launched itself at Sechral and the girl. Bowstrings twanged. Sechral flung Lae-Pinu flat along the shambri's back, threw himself across her. She felt the shambri stagger under the impact of the Drigg's attack and bleat in agony. Then she was falling, with Sechral's arms still holding her fast.

'Cut me loose, damn you!' Jerry raged. 'Cut me loose!' Helplessly he watched the pair roll clear of the mauled and drying shambri, saw the Drigg, studded with arrows, leap at them with bloodied jaws agape. On his knees, straddling the dazed girl, Sechral stabbed upwards with his spear. A thick, claw-tipped foreleg smashed the weapon aside, ripping one leather sleeve to gory ribbons. The black beast rose above him, snarling hideously. There was a great shout, and a stone spearpoint buried itself in the round, bristling head, transfixing the upper and lower jaws. Galdonn vaulted to earth, a long mace gripped in both broad hands. Evading the slashing claws, he swung the mace twice with ferocious skill. Bones snapped. The Drigg shuddered and fell.

'My thanks, brother.' Sechral rose, swaying. Sweat shone on his bloodless face. Dark streams coursed down his torn arm, spattering the silvery grey of Lae-Pinu's coveralls. He stooped, reaching down a hand to her. Galdonn waited. Sechral staggered, recovered his balance, looked vaguely at his brother, and then his knees buckled. Galdonn, grinning wolfishly, caught him and raised him from the ground as if he were a child.

'I will take him.' The voice was that of Chailemm. Galdonn stared straight into the eyes of the Alanga Speaker as he towered over the scene of death and pain.

As Chailemm began to dismount, Galdonn said: 'No, my father. He rides with me.'

'So be it. You have earned the right to decide.' Chailemm took the limp form of his youngest son, held him while Galdonn remounted. Then he gave him over to the other's care. Turning to Lae-Pinu, who was sitting up and regarding the stiff and bloody corpse of the Drigg with horrified wonder, he said: 'Now you, small one.' Gently and without any apparent effort, he lifted her to the saddle of his shambri. For the first time since the action had begun, Jerry relaxed. He looked about him. What had become of the balance of the Drigg pack? Amazingly, they had not come to the assistance of their fellow. Shreds of flesh, some with clumps of hair attached, were strewn along one side of the clearing. Of the Mahra and their pursuers, there was no other sign. A pack of individualists, thought Jerry. God help the Alanga – and us – if the Drigg had acted differently. Twelve, working in unison would have made mincemeat of our band, shambri included.

The riders formed up again, and they set off at an easy pace in deference to the wounded hunter. As Chailemm's mount passed him, Sechral gave Lae-Pinu the pale ghost of a smile. Jerry, riding at her other side, saw that she was weeping. He leaned over, perilously, and called: 'Do not upset yourself too much, Lae-Pinu. These people are tough. He'll get over it!'

She looked back at him out of brimming hazel eyes.

Between sniffs, she said huskily: 'I was thinking of the little Mahra!'

They rode on under the white face of Harn.

CHAPTER TWENTY-TWO

'You lie! You lie!' Borud-Brahn was on his feet, his ponderous body shaking with the intensity of his anger. He pointed a gnarled hand at Lae-Varka. 'It is a trick, a plot to usurp the authority of the Elders! Beya-Sev cannot be destroyed! The Great Judge protects us!'

Cries of approval sounded from the group of Sev-Kalan assembled in the Hall, cries that had a note of hysteria in them. Several people left their seats and threw themselves down at the foot of the platform, as if to be reassured by closer proximity to their fount of wisdom. Standing by the console, Lae-Varka spoke in controlled tones, but small muscles in his face and hands jerked and quivered.

'Old man, you are a fool. Your eyes show you plainly that disaster is upon us, but your brain is too withered to accept the truth. I am the servant of the Wall, and the Wall does not lie. Those who say otherwise reject the authority of the Great Judge. Do the Elders set themselves above the Guardian of Beya-Sev?'

'Does Lae-Varka set himself above the Council of the Elders?' snapped a small, sharp-faced man at the further end of the council table. 'How do we know that he offers the correct interpretation of the Great Judge's words?'

Panting, Borud-Brahn demanded: 'Tell us what is about to

destroy Beya-Sev – if you can. What is the exact nature of the catastrophe?'

'Tell us!' cried a woman in the audience, and the crowd took up her words as if responding to a cue. 'Tell us! Tell us, Voice of the Wall!'

Lae-Varka nodded, ignoring the agitated Elders. 'You shall be told, if the Great Judge is willing.' He sat down at the console desk again.

Time crawled by. The Sev-Kalan, audience and Elders alike, sat tensely in the yellow-lit cavern of the Judgement Hall, mutely waiting. Towering over all, the glittering instrumented precipice that was the controlling brain of the city shone a sombre and relentless light upon them. The console clicked. Lae-Varka pushed back his chair. For a moment he sat, head bowed. As a murmur began to rise in the Hall, he stood and once more faced the assembly. The harshness had gone from his voice, replaced by a curious note of resignation.

'Elders and citizens of Beya-Sev, the word of the Great Judge is this. An object of enormous mass approaches our world at a velocity beyond understanding. This object comes from the regions outside the atmosphere, where no life exists. When it enters the atmosphere, the Great Judge has calculated that it will create a disturbance sufficient to overthrow the walls of the city. That is our fate. There is nothing that can be done to prevent it.'

The brief silence that followed shattered before a torrent of words. Men and women streamed from the Hall, carrying the dread news to the sleeping city. Borud-Brahn rounded upon Lae-Varka.

'The outlander who came to us with his fantastic tale of other worlds has done this! Did he not say that he and his people could move bodies through the airless spaces, against all reason? You, Lae-Varka, you were responsible for his keeping. Your carelessness allowed him to escape! And now we must suffer!'

The accused man made no reply. From the outer chambers and galleries came a sudden clangour. It grew rapidly in volume, a metallic thunder as of giant hammer-blows, battering upon the barriers that sealed off the upper city from the darkness below!

'What in blazes is going on down there?' The man from *The New York Herald Tribune* squinted into the glare of an Indian sun, as wind from the whirling rotors overhead whipped his words away. Below, the shadow of the big United Nations helicopter rippled over the myriad heads of the crowd, like a flat dark fish over pebbles. The scrape and shuffle of innumerable feet, the babble of a thousand thousand voices, blended in a featureless, ascending roar. From the starboard viewport, the red-bearded correspondent of the Swedish *Aftonbladet* said, wonderingly: 'It looks like some kind of dance. But it's a pretty odd affair.'

'An example of contagion by communication.' The lanky *London Guardian-Times* representative spoke with his usual air of casual omniscience. Watching the slow, mindless whirlpool of human figures half-a-mile outside the Gandhi Space Launching Site's electrified fence, he continued: 'The four a.m. satellite relay brought scenes of dancing mania in Southern China and Brazil. Our friends down there, lacking anything more constructive to do, no doubt were caught up by the craze and have imitated what they saw on their screens. That's our twenty-first century Earth – one big cosy electronic madhouse.'

'Four a.m.?' said the technical expert from *Pravda*, brushing an ant off her white stretch-suit. 'Don't you *ever* go to bed? And what is "dancing mania", please?'

'We can go into question one later. As for question two, there are historical parallels for the spectacle we are witnessing. Europe in the Middle Ages, during the onset of the Black Death, is a good example. The Death – bubonic plague – killed millions and shattered the structure of European society. Strange cults, irrational and perverted, arose in its wake. One notable symptom was a compulsion to dance which gripped crowds, without reason, so that they danced until they fell through sheer exhaustion.'

'They are just going round and round and round,' exclaimed *Aftonbladet*. 'Thousands of them! Does anyone know the Skygrid count today?'

'Seven point four millions at 0800 hours,' the *Herald Tribune* newsman informed him. 'At that time, the robocopter had covered three-tenths of the perimeter. Then somebody blasted it down.'

'Seven million people in less than a third of the total distance around the field! And still they are arriving!'

'I do not see the relevance of the effects of the Black Death, I am afraid.' The tone of *Pravda's* remark was sceptical rather than apologetic.

'Me neither,' grunted *Herald Tribune*.

'To answer our colleague's very pertinent question,' said *Guardian-Times* reprovingly, 'I would refer you to the excellent United Nations summary of fifty years work upon the psychological effects of overcrowding. The Black Death has been eradicated, my friends, but Man has created a less tractable plague to replace it. Himself! The new scourge of humanity is – humanity.'

'Hey, hey! Who is that?'

Conversation ceased at *Aftonbladet's* cry. His eyes pressed to a binocular viewer, he was gesturing forward and down with one freckled, knuckly hand. Ahead, a colossal hemisphere swelled above the clustered tents and caravans, a dome as yellow as the sun and only a little less bright. The Master Chapel of the Church of Relativity was an imposing sight, not least because of the military neatness of the lesser installations surrounding it and isolating it from the antlike, swarming disorder of the multitude. But to the reporters it was a familiar landmark in their daily survey of the fantastic scene at the Launching Site. Something else had drawn *Aftonbladet's* attention. Peering through another viewer, *Herald Tribune* whistled. On the huge stage curving across the base of the dome stood a tall, regal, blonde-haired woman in her late fifties. A glittering cloth-of-gold kaftan draped her statuesque figure, a mass of necklaces and pendants hung with jewelled symbols encased her upper body. Men and women in plain yellow robes attended her, deferentially.

'That, kiddies,' announced *Herald Tribune*, 'Is Sophie Gavin, the power behind the throne of Relativity, no less!'

'She is the wife of Minister Gavin, the leader of the Church?' asked *Pravda*.

'Indeed she is,' said *Guardian-Times*, cutting in on *Herald Tribune*. 'Her younger sister, Kate, married the designer of *The Hope of Man*, which must make for some interesting chat at family reunions. I don't like the look of this at all. There's entirely too much Relativity heavy artillery, both literal and figurative, concentrated here. I hope Marshal Hira has a good intelligence service.'

'That's all for today, people.' The bored voice of the pilot signalled the end of the daily flight. The helicopter swung in a wide arc, across the sprawling, motley multitude encamped on the sunbaked plain, over the gleaming strands of the fence, into the airspace above the shimmering, sterile vastness of the silicon-concrete launching field. Behind them, the tall, glittering figure on the curved stage stared enigmatically at the glass towers of the Control Centre. The dance went on.

CHAPTER TWENTY-THREE

Harn was setting as the party of riders crossed the highest ridge of the hills and came in sight of the sea. So unexpected was the sight that Jerry's breath caught in his throat. Memory came back to him of the first view of the city and the plateau seen from the Control Room of *The Hope of Man*, of the suggestion of a coastline beneath an orange-tinted screen of clouds. The dark, rippling plain that curved along the horizon, broken by crests that glinted in the white light of the sinking planet, seemed part of a different order of reality. A cold night wind blew from it, sighing through the valleys and passes, tugging at the creaking branches of gnarled, tenacious trees. Near him, Sechral woke momentarily and moaned softly. Jerry looked at the young Alanga, slumped against the solid bulk of his elder brother.

'How is he, now?'

Galdonn turned, slowly. His square, bearded face regarded the Earthman for several seconds, as if he were assessing the motive behind the query. Finally, he said, gruffly: 'The wound is less deep than it appears. He will be well again soon.'

But Jerry read a different diagnosis in the unguarded flicker of Galdonn's eyes toward the injured man, even as he spoke. To hell with caution, he thought to himself, there's a man dying here. In a voice pitched to carry, he called: 'I have medicines which may cure his wounds, if you will permit me to use them. But we must return to my vehicle to recover them.'

Galdonn's features froze. Hostile glances were turned upon Jerry by the riders within earshot. Too weary and sore to care about possible consequences, he glared back at them with equal fierceness, silently cursing them for their super-stitious conservatism. Riding at his right, Lae-Pinu's expression was unreadable in the dying light. Chailemm sat massively in his saddle, seemingly not to have heard Jerry's words. The rider Genli, whose shambri Jerry shared, murmured: 'Speak not of the devices of science, stranger. If it is the will of Harn, the Speaker's son will recover.'

Now the trail dipped down into a steep-walled valley filled with shadow. Coldness welled up from the hidden depths, lapping about them like a rising tide. Jerry clamped his tongue between his teeth to keep them from chattering as the chill seeped into his aching muscles. He was dismally certain that he would be unable to walk or sit for at least a week, when this spine-jolting ordeal was over. The impulse to turn up the heating unit of his suit was almost irresistible, but he fought it down, knowing the importance of keeping his captors in ignorance of the nature of the garments worn by the girl and himself. Soon the rocky hillsides had shut off their view of the sea, and the last pale silver of Harn winked out. Through the intense blackness that followed, a glimmer of red began to emerge. It strengthened as they descended, and presently the smell of burning rose to Jerry's nostrils. At the same moment, a challenge rang out from the darkness.

'Who rides?'

Chailemm's voice boomed in reply. A robed figure, smudgily silhouetted by the distant fires, stepped into the trail. Bowing, the sentinel waved them onwards with a move-ment of the long spear which he carried.

The ground became mossy, the slope flattened out, and a

short while later they were following the course of a stream that trickled lazily across the valley floor, toward a group of stone huts. Smoke drifted to them on the breeze, underlaid with the rich scents of flowering vegetation. Jerry, his senses sharpened despite his weariness by the need to absorb new information, suddenly experienced a thrill of pure, cold horror. Out of the night air overhead rushed a winged something that swooped across his line of sight, an arm's length of less before him. He jerked away from the apparition, bringing an explosive curse from Genli as his shoulder thudded into the Alanga's chin. The flying thing flared its wings, checked, and settled to the left arm of Chailemm. Lae-Pinu squeaked, throwing herself backwards so abruptly that only the Speaker's great strength and reach prevented her from pitching headlong to the trail.

'Steady, now . . . steady,' Chailemm murmured. The girl, sitting as far from the new arrival as was possible, watched apprehensively as it extended downy forearms ending in tiny, almost vestigial hands, and clambered up the sleeve of the Speaker's robe to his shoulder. Seated there, it began to talk to him in a thin, piping voice. More of the creatures flew out of the darkness, settling to the arms of other riders. Only the one that came to Sechral did not alight, but flew continually about the shambri and its burden, emitting a keening whine that made Jerry's flesh creep.

'What are those things?' he asked of Genli.

'They are the chibba, the children of Harn,' said the Alanga, ruefully rubbing his bearded jaw. 'Once, long ago, they were mute, but Harn in his wisdom gave them the gift of speech. Now they guard our village at night, warning us of the approach of savage beasts.'

People crowded into the firelight as the band approached. Some, who had been sleeping in the clearing, awoke and stretched and arose to greet their kin. It seemed to Jerry that the whole adult community – he saw no children – had abandoned their rest to be present when the riders returned. To see a stranger, he wondered? How long had

139

they known of his presence *before* that encounter on the hillside?

They rode into the clearing. Women and slim girls with silver ornaments gleaming in their hair moved to greet their menfolk. Afterwards, their eyes turned in bold curiosity to the blond Earthman and the grey-clad figure of Lae-Pinu. A few elderly women tended cooking pots, a scattering of greybearded men squatted at the edge of the circle of warmth, looking on with sunken, indifferent faces. Through the crowd came a tall woman who walked with an athletic, yet wholly feminine, stride. She stood by Chailemm's shambri, surveying Lae-Pinu with bright blue eyes. The Speaker reached down and took her slim hands in his.

'Myrhial.' The tone was formal, the clasp affectionate. With equal gravity, the woman replied: 'Chailemm, my husband.'

Her keen gaze passed now to Jerry, and something prompted him to make a curteous bow, or something as close to a bow as his situation allowed. But when he looked up again, she was staring at something beyond him and her face had gone quite blank. As he dismounted, leaning heavily upon Genli, Galdonn walked by bearing the limp body of Sechral. Together with Myrhial and two of the Alanga, he entered the largest of the stone buildings and closed the door. As the silent procession disappeared, Jerry's attention was caught by a movement just out of range of the firelight. He glanced, casually, and then for an instant his heart seemed to stop.

A girl with red hair walked toward the fires, her long robes trailing on the damp moss. She walked as if asleep, guided by some inner sense rather than by cognizance of the outer world. Jerry, without conscious thought, ran to meet her.

'Cathy!' His voice broke the hush that had fallen upon the crowd. 'Cathy!'

Stumbling, slipping, hampered by his bound hands, he ran. Gasping, he halted before her, staring into the face that he knew better than any other in his personal universe. The familiar wide green eyes looked calmly back at him without sign of recognition.

'Cathy!' he cried, 'My God, what have they done to you?'

CHAPTER TWENTY-FOUR

Panic reigned in the Hall of Judgement. Bathed in the yellow gloom of the Wall, the Elders of the city were motionless, paralysed by a danger beyond their experience. On the floor of the vast room the ordinary citizens milled purposelessly, not knowing whether to flee or stay. The very air quivered to the crash and clang of beaten metal, waves of numbing sound that surged from the dim passageways converging upon the Hall. With each monstrous blow, fear mounted. In all the known history of the upper city of Beya-Sev, never had the gates and portals of the Sev-Kalan been so assailed. In all their lore, there existed no precedent for action in such a situation.

As if moving against some great pressure, Borud-Brahn, oldest of the Elders, took one lurching step toward the silent figure of Lae-Varka. The movement was contagious. As one man, his five colleagues rose to their feet. Spittle flecked Borud-Brahn's writhing lips. His outstretched hands clawed at Lae-Varka's throat, while unintelligible sounds of anger spilled from his mouth, thin and high against the brazen clangour from without. The Speaker for the Great Judge staggered under the attack, yet seemed unaware of what was happening. A concerted wail of dismay went up from the people below as they saw their leaders in disorder.

'Murderers! *Alabs*!' Screaming, a small, blonde-haired

woman ran up the steps of the dais. She hurled herself upon the broad back of Borud-Brahn, clawing at the Elder's distorted face. The five others milled around the struggle, seeking to tear her away from their senior spokesman. She cried out again, in a paroxysm of rage and fear.

'Husband, husband! They will kill you! Fight! Fight!'

Lae-Varka woke suddenly from his trance. With a growl, he clamped thick fingers about Borud-Brahn's wrists, and heaved. The Elder reeled back and fell heavily against the table. Without pausing, the Speaker drove into the remaining councilmen with clumsy, powerful blows. They scattered in confusion. Breathing heavily, he stood, shoulders hunched and head lowered, heedless of the woman's chattering reassurances. Tentatively, one of the five approached Borud-Brahn, and stooped over his unmoving bulk. Then he backed hastily away, a sick look upon his thin face.

'He is dead!'

The words were scarcely audible, but the Elders needed no further telling. Skirting widely the glowering presence of the Speaker, they streamed down the steps into the dazed and bewildered audience. A wild medley of cries arose:

'What shall we do? How can we protect ourselves against the Sev-Alab?' And loudest of all: 'Why does the Great Judge stay silent?'

Lae-Varka strode to the edge of the dais. His voice rang out over the clamour, stilling for a moment the aimless darting of the crowd. In fearful fascination they stared at the killer of Borud-Brahn.

'The Great Judge is silent because he has nothing more to say! The day of destruction has come upon Beya-Sev and the people must perish. Go, do whatever you wish, there is no one to check or counsel you. Your leaders, your Elders, are weak, tired old men, devoid of hope or wisdom. Go!'

Without waiting to observe the effect of his words, he turned back to the Wall. His wife laid a hand upon his arm, but he shook her off.

'Go with the others. There is nothing more here for you.'

She looked into his face as if it were the face of a stranger.

144

His eyes watched her from another world, through a curtain of yellow mist. He said, again: 'Go, woman. Save yourself if you can. If the Wall must cease, then there is no place for the Speaker, or need for sons.'

Roughly, he pushed her toward the steps. As she falteringly retreated, there came a terrible screeching of torn metal that transcended all previous sounds from the embattled gateways. A man's voice yelled hysterically: 'The barrier is broken! They are through!'

The crowd broke and fled, scurrying through arches and tunnels, scattering in a dozen directions. Alone with Borud-Brahn's corpse in the echoing vastness of the Hall, Lae-Varka walked unhurriedly to the console chair and seated himself.

CHAPTER TWENTY-FIVE

Tears blurred Jerry's vision. He reached out to cup Cathy's face in his bound hands, oblivious to the watching Alanga. His fingers, brushing aside a lock of auburn hair, touched a small, crooked scar, red against the fair skin at her temple. A flicker of pain broke the serenity of her gaze. And then, very slowly, awareness dawned. Her hands rose to touch his, warm on the numbed flesh.

'Je . . . rry?'

Scarcely breathing, he watched the transformation, saw the light brighten in her green eyes as memories linked to memories and the world became whole and coherent once more.

'Jerry!'

Standing amid the dismounted hunters, supported by Chailemm's solid bulk, Lae-Pinu saw the man and the girl embrace. Joy and bitterness filled her. She felt very small and cold and alone.

'The cure is complete.' The Alanga Speaker's deep voice held an unexpected warmth. He laid one huge hand gently on Lae-Pinu's shoulder. 'Come. You will need food, and a place by the fire.'

Limping as circulation returned to her newly-freed limbs, she allowed herself to be led to the central fire where it leaped and crackled within a circle of stone slabs. Liquid bubbled in a deep clay pot suspended above the flames. Strange, yet somehow appetising, smells arose from it. She sat down upon a rug of shambri hair and let the heat and the hypnotic flicker of firelight lull her fears.

Presently, Cathy and Jerry walked into the clearing. To Lae-Pinu it seemed that his face had lost the tense, almost gaunt look that she had known. Beside him paced Cathy in her robe of brown, tall as the tallest of the Alanga women, her hair glowing a rich and coppery red. As they approached, Chailemm rose, towering over the assembly. Seeing Lae-Pinu seated nearby, Jerry gave her a broad, cheerful smile. To Cathy he said: 'This is Lae-Pinu, who saved me from the biggest, gaudiest and most unpleasant computer ever built! I'll tell you all about it later!'

The English words were incomprehensible to the girl, but the tone of voice, and Cathy's warm greeting, brought an answering smile to her lips. With a faint feeling of envy she watched the Earthwoman pass on toward Chailemm with graceful, long-legged strides. Jerry said, as he halted before the Speaker: 'It seems that I have a lot to thank you for, in spite of our manner of meeting. But why did you not tell me that Cathy was alive? You must have guessed that she was the woman I sought.'

'Feelings are more truly revealed by actions, than by words,' the Alanga replied. He drew a long knife from his belt, and gestured at Jerry's bonds. 'I think we can trust you now! You were strangers, and your wife does not speak our language, and so we could not know your true intentions.'

The keen blade shore through the ropes. Jerry flexed his wrists gratefully, feeling the tingle of increasing circulation in his veins.

'You are right, of course,' he acknowledged. 'Did your hunters meet us by accident, or have you been watching our movements ever since we left the city? And where did you find my wife?'

Chailemm laughed. 'Too many questions after a long journey and with an empty stomach! Sit, Jericornelius and Cathy, and we will eat and talk.'

Women brought wooden bowls of hot, savoury stew and set  them before the Speaker and his guests. Jerry ate without qualms, knowing that Cathy had suffered no ill-effects during her time in the village. Lae-Pinu, however, stared in consternation at the peculiar brown liquid in which pieces of a strange substance floated, mixed with what were obviously the chopped stems and leaves of plants. *People* did not eat *plants*! But people obviously did, she told herself, as the others ate with evident enjoyment. Hesitantly she spooned up a portion, and took a tiny sip, unaware that a great many pairs of eyes were covertly watching her reactions. The first sip was followed by the spoonful, and she settled down to serious eating. Chailemm re-opened the conversation.

'We have observed your movements from the day that your fire-car descended, Jericornelius. Had it not been for the necessities of the hunt, we might have been present when you met the flying device, and so prevented you from being lured within the city. Returning to your trail, we traced the marks of your vehicle, but were too late to intervene. We glimpsed the flyer as it entered the city wall, and realised what had happened.'

Jerry translated this for Cathy's benefit. She smiled ruefully.

'Ill-missed by moonlight, to twist a phrase. But what I can't wait to know is – how did they get me out of the city? I can't remember the event very clearly, but it *must* have been the Alanga who saved me. There was –'

'The robot!' Jerry exclaimed interrupting her. 'Of course! That's who it was!'

Seeing her puzzled expression, he went on: 'During the struggle with the Sev-Alab, the city savages, I glimpsed a tall

149

figure in one of the corridors. It looked like the robot that admitted us to the city, but it must actually have been one of our friends here.'

When this exchange had been explained to Chailemm, he seemed to debate inwardly for some moments. Finally, he said: 'The ways into Beya-Sev are known only to the hunters, but I will tell you this much – the stream which flows from these hills becomes a river and disappears into the earth an hour's ride from the city walls. From this river, Beya-Sev draws its water, through many huge shafts. The people of the city have long forgotten the source of their water supply, and the fact that the shafts lead to the outer world.'

'But the people who *left* the city,' Jerry said, slowly. 'Remembered, or re-discovered, those ways.'

There was a longer pause. A certain tension had invaded the conversation. At last, Chailemm continued in an altered tone.

'You are shrewd. I see that you did not waste the time that you spent in Beya-Sev. Yet truth can be a potent weapon –'

He broke off as a dark-robed man moved quietly into the firelight and murmured something that Jerry did not catch. The Speaker nodded. Rising, he said to the three guests: 'I must leave you for a while. My people will see to your needs. Sleep well.'

He strode away toward the hut where Sechral lay wounded. Cathy turned to Jerry.

'What happened? The atmosphere went distinctly frigid there, just before he left.'

Jerry grimaced. 'That was your husband putting his foot in his big mouth. I made a guess at the relationship between the Alanga and the city people – their languages are almost identical – and Chailemm obviously thought me too sharp to be healthy. Now I think his son must have recovered consciousness and they've called him in. I'll watch my words from now on.'

'Speaking of words,' Cathy said. 'How have you become so fluent so suddenly in the native tongue? And how did you

150

acquire this very pretty child who thinks you are the greatest thing since Neil Armstrong?'

'Can I help it if I'm the father-figure type?' He grinned at her, and then said, soberly: 'From Lae-Pinu's point of view, poor kid, that's too true to be funny. Let's tell our respective stories, and see what sort of a picture of the situation we can make from them.'

They talked, with Jerry translating between Lae-Pinu and Cathy until the meal was over. The Alanga women and hunters spoke little to them, but were courteous enough. Afterwards, the women led Cathy and Jerry to an unoccupied hut that was clean and simply furnished, and took Lae-Pinu to share a room with the daughters of Genli. In the clearing the fires slowly dimmed.

Morning was brilliant, the sky a clear blue-green, the hills sharp and glistening with the pre-dawn rain. After a breakfast of fruit, the Terrestrials had climbed a winding flight of steps carved into the face of a steep slope, and stood now at the base of the most striking man-made object in the valley. Towering high above them, the rough-hewn stone figure of a robed man flung out its arms to the heavens. Craning his head to look at the sunlit torso and face, Jerry said: 'It was pretty dark when I rode in last night, but I must have been really asleep in the saddle to have missed *that*!'

'Jerry.' Cathy's voice was low but urgent. 'Jerry, look at this bas-relief!'

He looked at the area she indicated, a circular depression in the grey-green, crumbling face of the pedestal. As if to convince himself of the reliability of his vision, his fingers traced the raised edges of the map carved there. Then he and Cathy stood staring at each other while the songs and cries of the villagers rose faintly on the morning breeze, until Jerry said, almost in a whisper: 'It's all there, every curve and peninsula. My God, Cathy, that is a perfect, undeniable map of *Asia*!'

CHAPTER TWENTY-SIX

Speculation ran riot in Jerry's mind as he stood in the shadow of the huge Alanga statue, staring unseeingly at the sunlit hills and the distant green of the ocean. Near him, Cathy studied the enigmatic carving on the pedestal, moving from left to right as if a change in viewpoint might explain its uncanny resemblance to Earthly maps of Asia.

'It couldn't, perhaps, represent a land-mass on this planet?' She spoke tentatively, already aware of the answer.

Jerry shook his head.

'Not a chance, honey. We saw enough of the surface, as we orbited before landing, to be certain that there are no continents remotely like *that*.' He drew a deep breath. 'No, there's a beautifully simple explanation for the similarity. Except that it's weirder than anything we met in hyperspace –'

A girl's excited call cut across his words. Turning, he saw two young women in green robes, hurrying up the steep steps that led to the statue. There was something familiar about the appearance of the smaller of the pair.

'Why, it's Lae-Pinu!' Cathy exclaimed, laughing. 'She seems to have picked up local colour as quickly as I did! What is she shouting?'

'The Sev-Kalan equivalent of "Good morning!"' Jerry said. 'But I guess she has more than that to tell us.'

Holding up the trailing hem of her robe, Lae-Pinu ran

across the rock platform toward them. Breathlessly, she gasped: 'Cathee! Jeh-ree! I found her!'

'Steady, girl – take it easy! Who did you find?'

She reached for the hand of the taller girl, who had hung back. Pulling her forward, she said: 'This is my sister, Lae-Mura! She has become an Alanga! Isn't it fantastic?'

'Your older sister who was taken from Geya-Sev?' Jerry looked at Lae-Mura's yellow hair, at her huge dark eyes. 'Yes, I can see the family good looks. She's remarkably healthy for a girl who was sacrificed to an all-devouring god!'

Lae-Mura looked faintly puzzled. Lae-Pinu rapidly explained Jerry's joke, while he summarised the situation for his wife's benefit. Smiling now, Lae-Mura said: 'The legends that we were taught in Beya-Sev were tales to frighten children. The god of our people is Harn, the White One, who embraces all and in whom we are all one. Only under Harn is there life – the city is dead.'

Jerry was reminded of Lae-Pinu's little sermon on the virtues of the Food, in the prison in Beya-Sev. Cathy murmured: 'Ask her about the map. She may be less tight-lipped than Chailemm.'

'Good idea.' He indicated the weathered bas-relief. 'Lae-Mura, can you tell us what this carving represents? Is it some place known to the Alanga?'

She shook her head. 'I do not know. Such things are not the business of women. Perhaps the Speaker and the wise men of our tribe could tell you.'

'I might have guessed her answer, in this type of society,' commented Cathy, when the translation was made. She looked squarely at Jerry. 'You believe that it *is* Asia, don't you?'

'Yes. Incredible as it sounds, it seems even less probable to me that two completely distinct evolutionary processes could produce the degree of similarity that exists between ourselves and these people. I'm convinced that we've sprung from the same basic stock.'

'Yet how could . . .' Wonder shone in Cathy's green eyes. 'Hindu mythology! If only I had had more time to listen to

154

Hira on the subject. He was certain that there was a scientific basis underlying it all.'

As she concluded, there came sudden, concerted cries from the girls. Simultaneously, he saw that they had all acquired a second shadow, a shadow that swept swiftly from north to south like the hand of some sinister clock. Wordlessly, he stared at the sky. Along the horizon, the straggling remnants of the rain-clouds had been caught up, boiled, steamed into nothingness in the wake of a vast, fiery mass that rushed across the vault of the heavens. While the incandescent track of its passage still burned on their retinas, the sea exploded. There came an intolerable sound, a thunderclap that drove them to their knees, a sound that crushed into inaudibility the whole compass of normal noise, an inverted silence. Ripped apart as if by a monstrous knife, the waters leapt skywards in two jagged walls, bursting at their crests into million-ton masses of spray. Literally, the water shattered, its basic structure torn apart by the terrible impact of the shock wave. The firebolt swooped below the northern hills, outrunning its own thunder, trailing its cone of devastation over the edge of the world.

Jerry, with blood streaming from his nose and mouth, staggered to his feet just as the shock wave struck the coast-line. The rocks groaned and quivered. A thousand faults collapsed before the sudden pressure. Dust and fragments spurted as whole hillsides slid ponderously across their harder, deep-rooted foundations. Shielding his face with his arms, Jerry reeled blindly across the little plateau towards the huddled figure of his wife. Halfway to her, he collided with Lae-Pinu, who gripped his coveralls, yelling inaudibly. He swept her along with him in a tottering run to the base of the statue. Cathy, to his immense relief, sat up as they fell against the vibrating stone. Clinging desperately, each to the other, the three bowed their backs to the flying hail of rocks.

'Lae-Mura . . . Lae-Mura!' Lae-Pinu was screaming, but only now, at point-blank range, did her words reach Jerry. He cursed himself for forgetting the other girl. Raising his head, flinching at the scouring rasp of gritty particles across his face, he squinted into the storm. She was there, only yards away, crawling with infinite slowness across the plateau, the neck of her gown drawn over her head, protectively. He pushed away from the pedestal, ready to grab her. And then the sky fell. Or so his battered senses told him. A hurricane roared out of nowhere and in a split second the world vanished behind a cataract of salt rain. Lightning glazed and slashed through the downpour. The dust became mud, sliding from the hillsides in glutinous torrents.

A thunderous crack smote Jerry's ears. He looked upwards, one arm across his forehead, warding off the rain. In the eerie green flare of the lightning, he saw the trunk and head of the statue topple slowly outwards, arms spread wide as if in a final benediction over the valley below. There was nothing he could do to help the others. He crouched in the rain, shaking. The statue crashed over the plateau's edge and disappeared in the murk.

CHAPTER TWENTY-SEVEN

The machines had broken through. The upper city, citadel, of the Sev-Kalan, had fallen. Behind the grinding, clattering monsters that once had built the walls of Beya-Sev and maintained those walls for unreckoned centuries, the mindless hordes of the Sev-Alab poured in to ravage and destroy. Only the gigantic, brooding presence of the Great Judge struck some measure of fear into their cloudy, slow-moving minds, so that they still hesitated to approach the dais upon which a lone living man stood. The man was all but unaware of them. He had questions yet to ask. His thick fingers glided over the console.

Great Judge, why did you not warn your people of the arrival of the strangers in their fireship?

THE SOCIETY OF BEYA-SEV IS STAGNANT. IT SEEMED INTERESTING TO OBSERVE THE EFFECT OF NEW IDEAS AND TECHNOLOGY UPON ITS STRUCTURE. THE SURVIVAL POTENTIAL OF THE STRANGERS WAS ALSO OF INTEREST.

Then they are truly the cause of our overthrow! But why, Guardian of the City, have you abandoned your people to the beasts of the lower levels?

BECAUSE THE NEED FOR VIGILANCE IS GONE. MY PURPOSE IS FULFILLED. EVENTS HAVE MOVED BEYOND THE SCOPE OF THE POWERS

157

GIVEN ME BY MY CREATORS, YOUR ANCESTORS. BEYA-SEV MUST DIE. THE LONG SICKNESS HAS BITTEN TOO DEEP.

The long sickness?

THERE IS LITTLE TIME FOR EXPLANATION. SUFFICE IT THAT THE AIRLESS REGIONS BEYOND THIS WORLD ARE FILLED WITH FORCES INIMICAL TO LIFE.

Desperately, Lae-Varka pleaded: The airless regions? Great Judge, I do not understand. What has this to do with the Sev-Kalan?

KNOW THIS, THAT THE SHIP OF THE STRANGERS WAS THE SECOND SHIP TO LAND UPON BEYA.

Death came before his mind could grapple with the implications of the Wall's final statement.

On a broad ledge overlooking the plain, Cathy and Jerry stood beside the carrier, gazing at the smoking ruins of Beya-Sev. The light of a new morning cast an orange tint upon the towering, billowing black clouds that cast their gloom across plain and hill. At intervals, a white brilliance would lance upwards from the tumbled stones, followed by the crackle and rumble of unguessable energies breaking free of some buried mechanism, the sound carrying clearly over the intervening miles. The handful of Alanga riders assembled on the slopes above the ledge muttered in awed tones and fought the restless stirrings of their alarmed shambri. Jerry said, bleakly: 'When I first encountered Chailemm, I spun him a story of coming disaster, because I thought it might save my neck, and Lae-Pinu's. Well, it came true, and it's won our release, but I don't feel proud of being a prophet.'

'Don't talk is if it was your fault.' Cathy turned her eyes from the sombre spectacle to look at his troubled face. 'Space is full of wandering bodies, within planetary system such as this one. Earth was struck time and again in the past. The Alanga valley, I can see, must have caught only the outer fringe of the shock-wave. Beya-Sev was obviously on the direct path of destruction.'

'Yes, but was the fall of this planetoid a natural disaster – or was it induced?' Jerry's voice was pitched low, as if the nearby watchers might somehow grasp the meaning of his words despite their ignorance of his language. 'We've stirred up forces in this area of Space, willingly or otherwise, that could have effects beyond our knowledge. And beyond our ability to put right.'

'Darling, it's too late now to think like that. We are part of this world now, just as much as Chailemm or Lae-Pinu.' Cathy glanced at the small, robed figure standing forlornly apart from the group, face turned to the ruins of her home. 'What we must do now is to give the Alanga the help that we promised. This catastrophe has broken their old aversion to science by overwhelming their society with more demands for action than it can possibly meet. And there is no doubt, Jerry, that their community was dying, in the long view. Think of all those empty, decaying huts we saw, and the fact that there was actually another Alanga village, maybe more, somehere in the hills, according to the tribal lore. All gone, now.'

He sighed. 'I know, Cathy, I know. We've learned more about Chailemm's people since the disaster than we might otherwise have learned in a lifetime. The fact, particularly, that after fleeing from Beya-Sev centuries ago, they were forced to make perilous trips into the city to carry off girls because the numbers of their tribe were declining year by year – that's a clear enough indication of racial decay, when added to my own observations within the Sev-Kalan community. But it doesn't make that mess out there any easier to take.'

Chailemm's great voice boomed across the hillside, amid a chorus of fear and amazement from the riders.

'The fire-car returns! See, Jericornelius, where it falls!'

'It's ture, Jerry, it's true!' Cathy fairly yelled, pointing at the northern sky. High, high above glittered a point of light that grew as it fell, sliding down an intangible wire to meet the ponderous mass of the spinning planet. Jerry, too, began to shout. He hugged Cathy to him, and in another moment they had swept up the startled Lae-Pinu and were hustling her into the seat of the carrier. Calling to the hunters to follow, he

eased the vehicle into motion. But only the Speaker and Genli rode with him. The others remained, bunched on the hillside, an apprehensive group.

The Hope of Man made an impeccable touchdown not far from the stream that bordered the hills. Foam-jets spurted, laying the fires that sprang up around her stern, so that the wheels of the carrier made a gritty crunching as they braked within her shadow. The airlock was open, the silvery metal stairway extended itself to meet the travellers. And that was all.

'Where's Frank?' Cathy said, tensely. 'Jerry, do you think this is some sort of trap?'

Jerry stepped from the carrier.

'There's only one way to find out!'

He picked up the neurogun, gripped Cathy's hand briefly, and began to climb the stairway.

CHAPTER TWENTY-EIGHT

'So Minister Gavin stopped a slug,' the *Guardian-Times* man observed brightly, over the breakfast table. Looking at him sourly, *Herald Tribune* growled, through a mouthful of toast: 'Every damned thing around Gandhinagar City happens at four a.m. and you're always awake to see it!'

'Three a.m.,' said *Pravda* and then went as pink as her leather leotards.

To cover her confusion, *Guardian-Times* held out his cigarette-case and murmured: 'Have a Spinrad – the hay that makes the day!'

She smiled faintly at his burlesque of a current television commercial, but shook her head.

Spooning up yoghurt, *Aftonbladet* enquired: 'Do you think there is any substance to the Relativity people's claim that Hira had him assassinated?'

'Complete nonsense!' said *The Times of India* sharply. 'The Marshal is a man of peace. He would never countenance such an action.'

'Could be that removal of the Church of Relativity's head is the least bloody method of paralysing the body,' countered *Herald Tribune*. 'Hira may reckon the death of one man a small price to pay for the preservation of peace. We all know that Gavin controlled the most effective force in opposition to the whole starship project. Maybe he's crazy, maybe not, but his organisation is laser-razor.'

'Is *what*?' asked *Aftonbladet*.

'Sharp,' explained *Guardian-Times*. 'And the tense is incorrect. Controls, not controlled. The Minister's death has yet to be confirmed. In the meantime, his capable wife will –'

Heavy footsteps interrupted him. Major Armstrong loomed in the doorway, his tanned, heavy-jawed face grim. A pistol hung at his hip. With a perfunctory nod of greeting, he said: 'Until the present emergency is over, all flights have been cancelled to avoid provoking hostile reactions from the crowds at the perimeter. There are no, repeat no, exceptions to this order. Anyone contravening it will be severely dealt with. The usual television communication facilities will be available until further notice.'

Blast rattled the windows. White smoke boiled on the launching field, startingly close. Major Armstrong wheeled about, strode swiftly from the room. The correspondents crowded to the windows, breakfast forgotten.

It was like coming home after a long absence, only to discover tiger tracks in the living-room. Jerry prowled the corridors of *The Hope of Man*, neurogun at the ready, his senses almost painfully alert. Where was Frank Marek? A vivid mental picture presented itself of the stocky scientist crouching, laser pistol in hand, beyond the next corner. The thought was not pleasant. When he reached the first of the communication screens and activated it, he was surprised at the steadiness of his fingers.

The screen, connected to the Control Room, showed it to be empty. Good. From there, it would be possible to monitor every portion of the ship's interior. Jerry moved towards the central elevator, then paused. Supposing Marek knew where he was? Supposing he jammed the cage where he could pick Jerry off at his leisure? Steady on, son, he told himself, that sort of thinking fills graves. But he went away from the elevator and set himself to climb the vertical ladders.

On the plain, the city burned, intermittently spouting white  fire and shattered stone in a manner that made any thought of a close approach futile. Cathy's attention jumped from city to ship and back again, until she could bear the tension no longer. Watched by a wondering Lae-Pinu, she searched for, and found, her laser pistol and tucked it into her belt. Then, with a reassuring smile to the now alarmed girl, she headed for the starship's airlock, thankful that she had discarded the Alanga robes for the freedom of her flexible, close-fitting coveralls. Chailemm and Genli watched her go, but whatever doubts may have passed through their minds, their bearded faces remained impassive.

'The computer room, Cathy. Come in – there's no danger.'

She started as Jerry's voice boomed from a loudspeaker directly above her head. Then, realising that he must have observed her entrance on the monitor screens, she relaxed with a sigh of relief. Ascending rapidly to the upper sector of the ship, she came to the open doorway of the computer room. Stepping through, she saw Frank Marek. Instantly her lingering fears melted into compassion.

'Catherine, m'dear . . .' The voice was a thin parody of his old sardonic rasp. He lay against the opposite wall, supported by Jerry, regarding her with bright, drugged eyes. Cathy's medical training told her, even then, that they could do little for him. Kneeling, she took one of his bruised, bloodied hands in hers. She said, gently:

'Don't talk Frank. Just rest. We'll get you to your cabin and fix you up.'

Marek gave a wheezing laugh. 'I can die here . . . just as well as . . . in bed. Let me tell . . . you . . . what happened.'

She glanced at Jerry. He gave an almost imperceptible nod.

'Go ahead, Frank. Take it slowly.'

'Thank God you aren't . . . crying. Can't stand . . . snivelling . . .'

His voice dropped. For a moment his eyes seemed to lose focus. Then: 'Didn't want to live . . . saw things in hyperspace that should have stayed . . . buried. Took ship up again to . . . throw her into hyperspace close to sun . . . destroy her and myself.'

A trickle of blood ran down his chin. Cathy wiped it away. His flesh was icy against her fingers.

'Thanks . . .' His free hand began to work at a crease in his coveralls, back and forth, obsessively. 'Hyperspace . . . threw us out at Phase One . . . distortion caused by presence of . . . stellar . . .'

There was a long pause. Marek rallied, went on.

'Asteroid on collision orbit with ship as we . . . emerged into normal space. Atomic screen . . . vaporised part of it, but too massive to be . . . completely destroyed. Ship had to decide . . . collide or take . . . evasive action. Made course change . . .'

He was fighting for breath, Cathy, unable to watch any longer without making some gesture of help, began to reach for the medical kit lying nearby, unsealed. Marek gasped: 'Waste of time, girl . . . ship swung . . . I was in free fall . . . hit bulkhead . . .'

Jerry winced. Human flesh, floating weightless within the confines of *The Hope of Man*, driven suddenly like a slingshot against steel and plastic – he crushed the thought as Marek spoke again.

'Shook the kinks out of . . . my brain. Crawled here, cut off most functions of computer except those needed to . . . land ship. Watch computer, Jerry. All filled up with . . . crazy stuff I saw in hyper . . . hyper . . .'

He was dead. Jerry straightened, and they stared at each

other across Marek's broken body. Finally, Jerry said: 'It looks as if we have a lot of work ahead of us. Let's start now.'

CHAPTER TWENTY-NINE

Lae-Pinu stood on the hillside, watching the shadow of *The Hope of Man* lengthen across the misty plateau. The light of the sinking sun turned the titanium hull to a pillar of fire, burning against the purple of the darkening sky. Close by the ship, dwarfed by her vast, baroque architecture, Cathy and Jerry Cornelius paused for a moment before leaving the soil of a once alien world. Shading her eyes against the orange glow, Cathy surveyed the marching hills patchworked with scrub and forest, the faint light in the air above them that hinted of the hidden sea.

'Strange,' she said, slowly. 'I feel the sense of parting so much more strongly than when we left Earth.'

'I feel that, too.' Jerry's gaze followed hers to where the Alanga were gathered, a dark blur in the deepening dusk. One figure stood apart from the rest on the distant slope. 'In the four weeks since the meteorite fell, we've become involved with the people of Beya in a way which has no real counterpart on Earth. At least, not for anyone in our sort of profession. God knows, we owed them all the help we could give. I'll never stop wondering if *The Hope of Man* deflected that meteorite *towards* Beya, or if it actually helped to soften an already inevitable collision by vaporising part of the meteorite's mass.'

'Yes . . .' A shadow crossed Cathy's face. 'If my observations are correct, the Alanga and the Sev-Kalan were doomed from the beginning in a more insidious way. A war with unknown weapons, fought in some lost era of Asian history – a voyage across four light-years in a spaceship travelling at sub-light velocities . . . who knows? Exposure to radiation, at any rate, whether man-induced or present in space, setting up a slow decay, a long sickness . . .'

Jerry put one arm about her shoulders. 'Come on, honey. Let's go, before we both break down! We're leaving one person, at least, happier than before.'

Cathy smiled. 'That's true. I have a feeling that the next ship reaching Beya will be met by the new Mrs Sechral!'

They gave a parting wave to the far-off watchers.

Smoothly, the stairway folded itself into the hull as they entered the airlock. The airlock door slid shut.

Lae-Pinu waited until the last whisper of the spaceship's thunder faded across the plateau and the brilliant jet of nuclear fire merged with the appearing stars. Then, shivering, she began to climb the dark hillside to where the Alanga sat silently.

The cities of Earth were burning. In the bomb-scarred tower of Central Control, Marshal Hira studied the television screen's melancholy tally of death and destruction. New York had a million dead, Calcutta was a roaring pyre, London a battlefield . . . he blinked, angrily, as scenes and statistics merged and blurred before his weary eyes. How long since he had really slept? He couldn't remember. The world's hopes, the world's fears, had been wound too tightly, and restraint had snapped. If *The Hope of Man* did not return, would there ever be an end to the carnival of madness?

He straightened as the announcer said: 'A bulletin from the Church of Relativity states that Minister Gavin, shot by an unidentified attacker several weeks ago, is still in a coma. His condition worsened last night, and –'

Hira switched off. Another day had begun. He left for the main conference room to map out another twenty-four hours' strategy. With luck, they would have that long.

Six levels lower down, *Herald Tribune* grunted in surprise as he trained a binocular viewer on a small helicopter hovering over the yellow dome of the Church of Relativity.

'Look at this! Kate Bell dropping in on her sister Sophie Gavin, with her husband at the controls!'

'That's Alex Bell, sure enough,' said *Aftonbladet*. 'I wonder what he and his wife are after?'

'Waiting for his ship to come in,' answered *Guardian-Times*, appearing in the doorway in a scarlet dressing-gown. 'Are there two cups of coffee left? Oh, good!'

Beyond the orbit of Pluto, in the outermost darkness of the Solar System, a space-station floated its electronic senses turned always to the illimitable black gulfs between the stars. It had been built to respond to one signal only, the first that Man would send from interstellar space. It had waited a long time, but it was incapable of weariness or boredom. When the signal came, it began methodically to relay it to the worlds of men, close to the Sun.

'Proceed with landing,' Hira said. 'The field is clear. I repeat, the field is clear.'

He couldn't stop shaking. It had seemed that nothing could be worse than the long weeks without news, while *The Hope of Man* voyaged to unknown regions and strange planets, but the period that had elapsed since the robot station signalled her return had been sheer hell. Without Kate Bell, who had persuaded her sister that the Church would suffer as grievously from the violence it sought to provoke, as had its leader from a nameless gunman, the landing field would have been swamped by a sea of bodies. He rose now, unsteadily, and went to meet the descending ship.

The smell was overpowering. Cathy stood at the head of the stairway, averting her face from the breeze that blew over the field, carrying the stench of twenty million human beings and their refuse. Jerry sniffed.

'At times like this, I can appreciate Frank's point of view!'

'Poor Frank,' Cathy said, softly. 'The first victim of hyperspace. With the knowledge we gained on the return trip, it should be possible to make things easier for the colonizing ships.'

'Let's hope so.' Jerry took her hand. 'Here comes Hira and the gentlemen of the Press. Well, we can tell them that there is a new Earth out there, a clean Earth.'

Together they began to descend the stairway.

He added: 'And may they make better use of it than we made of the old one!'

MICHAEL MOORCOCK

WARRIOR OF MARS

That first visit to Mars had been a mistake. A miraculous journey out through the myriad miles of space and back, back through the millennia to a time before Man existed, it had been the chance result of a small-scale malfunction in an experimental matter transfer machine.

But Michael Kane's first great adventure in a world where great mythic armies battled, where hugely bizarre creatures roamed and deeds of high heroism and dark treachery resounded, was but the start. For as he learned to control and use the machinery, he was to return to Mars again and again.

For the first time in paperback, the complete Martian adventures of Michael Kane, of the proud Princess Shizala, her warrior brother and the darkly beautiful but evil Horguhl, are brought together in one volume.

A Royal Mail service in association with the Book Marketing Council & The Booksellers Association.

Post-A-Book is a Post Office trademark.

MICHAEL MOORCOCK

THE WAR HOUND AND THE WORLD'S PAIN

The forest flourished, a lush and spreading refuge from the Wars, coolly green and welcoming.

Beyond its borders the land burned flame red, blood red, ghastly black. Men and women, hacked to death, choked the paths and streams as the Armies of Religion clashed and slaughtered. Carrion-hung gibbets loomed starkly through the smoke and all the land was desolate.

The forest was a refuge. Yet silent, utterly silent and without life, as through it wearily rode the War Hound, Graf Ulrich von Bek. To come suddenly on a castle. Many-turreted and fair, it rose up, honey-gold in the sunlight. Yet silent and still as the forest.

And in the castle he found favour of the chatelaine, the Lady Sabrina, whose Master was Lucifer, Prince of Darkness. And was challenged to set out upon a quest that only the Damned could undertake.

HODDER AND STOUGHTON PAPERBACKS

MICHAEL MOORCOCK

THE RUSSIAN INTELLIGENCE

Jerry Cornell was a Class A Secret Agent.

Dedicated, Intrepid, Ice-cool in a Crisis, Resourceful, Master of Disguise, Impervious to Pain – by these qualities are such men known.

Jerry Cornell was different. He was honest – at least, to himself. He knew the truth: his trade wasn't glamorous, was hardly ever important, getting one side to defect to the other was a PR matter and most secrets aren't worth keeping anyway.

But, and these were important buts, it was fashionable. Camp even. Above all it offered wonderful opportunities for skiving and fiddling and marital infidelity.

Realist and coward, Jerry Cornell was doing very nicely. Until the terrible night when he found *The Devil Rider – Masked Fighter for Justice* and comic-strip hero clutched in the dying hand of a fellow agent Jerry had never much liked anyway . . .

HODDER AND STOUGHTON PAPERBACKS

MICHAEL MOORCOCK

THE RITUALS OF INFINITY

Outside time, outside space, the planets hung in limbo.

One was all desert, one covered in freshwater oceans, one in grey volcanic dust. Jungle covered another. Fifteen planets in all, each called Earth and each under threat.

Once upon a time there had been twenty-four alternate Earths, all similar, but one by one they had broken down in space dust and oblivion. And men had done this: the mysterious D-squads who travelled through subspace, attacking, de-stabilising, destroying . . .

Now one man stood between them and the total planetary break-up: Dr Faustaff, brilliant, overweight, Buick-driving, Hawaiian-shirted, space-commuting, always-on-call, Earth repair man and physicist. Who was 'Frisco-bound with a hitch-hiking redhead when the first off-Earth Emergency call came in . . .

HODDER AND STOUGHTON PAPERBACKS